'All right, Je

Findlay murmure
his voice made h
to her dismay, that his own deep blue eyes were
glittering with unshed tears.

'Findlay! Oh, Mr d'Arc, what is it?' she asked
anxiously.

'It's all right, little Jenny, it's nothing you've
said or done. You've just made me think of
another time, that's all. Someone I loved
deeply, and lost…'

Margaret Holt trained as a nurse and midwife in Surrey, and has practised midwifery for thirty-five years. She moved to Manchester when she married, and has two graduate daughters. Now retired and widowed, she enjoys writing, reading, gardening and supporting her church. Margaret believes strongly in smooth and close co-operation between obstetrician and midwife for the safe care of mothers and their babies.

Recent titles by the same author:

DOCTOR ACROSS THE LAGOON
REMEDY FOR PRIDE
AN INDISPENSABLE WOMAN

TALL, D'ARC
AND TEMPTING

BY
MARGARET HOLT

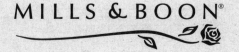
MILLS & BOON®

To my sister, Jenny Bennett Taylor,
with happy memories of Lyme Regis!

*First published in Great Britain 1998
Harlequin Mills & Boon Limited,
Eton House, 18-24 Paradise Road, Richmond, Surrey TW9 1SR*

© Margaret Holt 1998

ISBN 0 263 80800 9

*Set in Times Roman 10½ on 12 pt.
03-9806-48598-D*

*Printed and bound in Great Britain
by Mackays of Chatham PLC, Chatham*

CHAPTER ONE

'GOOD heavens! Nothing like being chucked in at the deep end,' muttered Jenny Curtis, her wide brown eyes taking in the little operating theatre where the Tuesday gynaecology list was scheduled for that morning, with a new visiting consultant surgeon and a new theatre sister: herself.

Apart from having briefly met the genial Irish GP who regularly gave the anaesthetics, the members of the team were complete strangers to her, as unfamiliar as this little country hospital itself—the very last place she would have chosen to gain work experience.

But, of course, it was not to further her career prospects that Jenny was now on the staff of Stretbury Memorial Hospital, a picturesque building in warm yellow Cotswold stone. It had been built by old Lord Hylton after the First World War, in memory of his son, for the inhabitants of the small Gloucestershire market town, and over seven decades it had expanded to include a well-equipped health centre from which a team of general practitioners covered a wide rural area.

In the 1960s the founder's granddaughter had endowed the Hylton annexe for twenty elderly residents, and these now included Jenny's grandfather, Will Curtis.

'You've got something to answer for, Grampy,' murmured Jenny as she began to prepare the theatre. It would be about an hour before the surgeon and his assistant arrived from Bristol, a fifteen-mile drive, but

Jenny wanted to be ready and waiting when they appeared. She had changed into a blue cotton theatre dress and plimsolls, and tucked her cropped brown hair under a blue elasticated paper cap. She checked the lights, especially the shadowless lamp over the operating table, the diathermy and suction pump.

She turned to the autoclaved packs on the shelves: operation sets, towels, dressings, plastic bowls and receivers; then the intravenous sets, the plastic litre and half-litre bags of saline, dextrose and Hartmann's solution; the suturing materials, needles and skin-clips; the surgeons' gowns and gloves. What size would this visiting man require? Jenny had no idea.

'Morning, Sister Curtis! My, you're an early bird!'

A smiling woman of about forty appeared in theatre blue, and introduced herself as Doreen Nixon, staff nurse on the women's ward and regular 'runner' for the weekly operation list.

'There's an auxiliary, Jill, who'll be here at eight-thirty,' she said. 'She assists Dr McGuire with the anaesthetics, and helps to wheel patients in and out, besides being at everybody's beck and call in the theatre.' She paused and eyed Jenny speculatively.

'Have you any idea what this new man's like, Sister? Jill and I are dying to know! You see, Mr Steynes has done these Tuesday lists for so long it's difficult to imagine anybody else in his place. And, of course, Sister McGuire was such a super—er—'

She broke off in embarrassment, and Jenny grinned.

'OK, Doreen, you were about to say that Mr Steynes and Sister McGuire were the greatest theatre duo the world has ever known, but now you and Jill have got to put up with two alien beings from the Planet Zog, and—'

'Oh, *no*, Sister, I didn't mean anything like that,' protested Doreen, relieved that Jenny was not offended. 'And, in any case, we've still got Dr McGuire as anaesthetist—you'll like him, he's a scream.'

'Good, 'cos I might want to scream along with him,' replied Jenny darkly, adjusting the overhead lamp and gauging where she would place the instrument trolley, the Mayo tray, the sterile water bowls on their stand and the two soiled-dressing containers.

This has to be the smallest theatre I've ever squeezed into, she thought. When Mr What's-his-name and his assistant are in here with the patient on the table, and Dr McGuire with the anaesthetic trolley, and Doreen and the all-purpose Jill running round in circles, I can't see that there's going to be space for *me* anywhere. Ah, well!

She smiled to herself, lifting her firm chin and remembering the patients whose lives would be in the surgeon's hands on this bright and sunny April morning—the women who might be full of fear, whose families could be dreading the outcome of today's findings. These, after all, were the ones that mattered, and Jenny was resolved to do her best for them.

The first hour sped by rapidly. Jill arrived and busied herself in the little adjacent room from where Dr McGuire could be heard whistling 'Flowers o' Donegal'. Jenny put on a surgical mask and began to scrub up at the long wash-basin. Drying and powdering her hands, she thrust them into the sleeves of the green theatre gown that Doreen held up for her, and pulled a pair of size 6 sterile rubber gloves over the cuffs.

She started setting out the towels, instruments and dressings on the trolley, while Doreen poured antiseptic lotion into a bowl and opened sterile envelopes of suturing thread, dropping the contents into a tray at one corner of the trolley. Jenny became absorbed by the familiar routine, and did not look up when two men entered, dressed in blue theatre T-shirts, trousers and caps, and wearing white surgical boots.

'*Jenny*!'

The younger man's voice caused Jenny to spin round and gasp in amazed delight.

'*Steve*! Oh, what a lovely surprise—I had no idea that you'd be—er, good morning, sir,' she added towards the tall figure standing behind Dr Steve Forrest, the obs and gynae house officer at the large Bristol teaching hospital that Jenny had so recently left.

'Good morning, Sister.' The new consultant nodded to her and Doreen, then towards the glass panel where Jill's face could be seen peering through. 'Perhaps Dr Forrest will introduce us before we start the list.'

Steve gave Jenny an imperceptible wink as he replied, 'Certainly, sir. Jenny, this is Mr d'Arc—Mr Findlay d'Arc, who has just begun a locum consultancy in obstetrics and gynaecology. And this is Sister Jenny Curtis who will be assisting us.'

'With nurses Nixon and—er—Jill,' added Jenny quickly. 'Dr McGuire is anaesthetising our first patient, sir, and will bring her in as soon as you are ready for her. Dr McGuire is one of the four general practitioners based at the health centre here, and was an anaesthetic registrar at—'

'Thank you, Sister,' the consultant broke in firmly. 'By the end of the morning we shall be better acquainted, no doubt.'

His deep voice held a faint trace of an accent which Jenny was unable to place—could it possibly be French?

Steve grinned and then raised his eyebrows at Jenny, signalling that he found d'Arc's formality rather heavy going. Her spirits had lifted at the unexpected sight of the fair-haired, boyish-faced houseman with whom she had worked at Bristol, and they exchanged smiles over the tops of their masks while Doreen assisted the men into sterile green gowns and tied the tapes at the back.

'Oh, heavens, Mr d'Arc, yours is too short on you!' exclaimed Doreen, hastily tracing her finger down the pile of packaged gowns to find a larger size.

'It will do, Nurse,' he said, glancing down at the hem that barely covered his blue-trousered knees. 'Maybe you can find a longer one for the next operation. Right, Sister, are we ready with Mrs Norma Pritchard? Menorrhagia, for hysterectomy.'

Jenny noticed that he was familiar with the patient's name, even though he was a stranger to them all. The door opened, and Dr McGuire wheeled in the blissfully unconscious Mrs Pritchard, complete with an intravenous drip. Two wooden poles were slid through each side of the canvas sheet on which she lay. Dr McGuire took hold of both poles at the top end and Doreen and Jill each took a pole at the bottom end to lift her across to the operating table.

The consultant frowned. 'It's no wonder that nurses strain their backs. You don't have a patient slide here?'

The two nurses looked blank, and Jenny quietly explained to them that most large theatres now used a wide, rigid plastic sheet that slid under the patient and across the operating table as she lay beside it. A gentle push slid her smoothly across from the trolley to the table, and vice versa.

'I shall ask if we can have one for next week, sir.'

'Good. Like many excellent ideas, it is so simple,' Mr
d'Arc replied, glancing at Mrs Pritchard's case-notes
which Jill had placed on a special shelf. 'Read me the
number on her wrist-band, please, Nurse.'

Jill did so, and Mr d'Arc then asked to see the consent
form from the case-notes.

'Thank you, Nurse. I see that her husband has also
signed. Very well, Sister, are you ready? Swabs
counted?'

'Yes, sir.' Jenny took a pair of sponge-forceps and
painted Mrs Pritchard's abdomen with pink antiseptic
dye. After arranging sterile towels around the area, she
handed Mr d'Arc the scalpel, with a new blade attached,
to make the horizontal incision. Steve stood by with artery forceps, and as soon as the pelvic cavity was opened
Jenny handed Mr d'Arc the large abdominal retractor
which would stay in position throughout the operation.
He examined the pelvic organs carefully.

'The uterus has multiple fibroids, and I shall remove
it,' he said. 'Many surgeons would remove her ovaries,
too, but she is not yet fifty, and they could still possibly
be of some use to her. Everything else appears
healthy—bladder, rectum, lymph nodes—yes. Very well,
Sister, let's have the abdominal swabs, dissectors, scis-
sors— Is the aspirator on?'

Jenny swung the Mayo tray round on its stand so that
the consultant could help himself to the instruments he
needed immediately. A familiar surge of exhilaration
swept over her, the stimulus of being involved in a
highly skilled procedure.

Gone was the uncertainty, the apprehension that had
hung over her earlier, and she found herself enjoying
every moment, anticipating the surgeon's moves and re-

quirements in smooth, unhurried co-ordination. He worked at an even pace, deftly and cleanly, occasionally murmuring a request and always following it with a word of thanks. It was perfect teamwork.

Once the vital part of the operation had been completed Steve Forrest relaxed a little and raised his eyebrows at Jenny across the table.

'And 'ow do 'ee reckon 'ee'll take to country loife, me dear?' he asked in an exaggerated Gloucestershire burr. 'It be a big change from they city loights, oo-ah!'

'Give me time, Dr Forrest. I only started work here yesterday,' she replied in a low tone. She was preparing the sutures, threading lengths of catgut onto stitch-holders.

'I heard you were to be in charge of the men's ward here,' he continued.

'I am, but I was asked to take the Tuesday gynae list and deputise as general relief sister. The men's ward has only ten beds, mainly post-operatives transferred from Bristol hospitals to be nursed nearer to their homes.'

'Ten beds! Who's in charge of the whole set-up, then?'

Jenny glanced at Dr McGuire who was adjusting the flow of nitrous oxide through the intratracheal tube.

'Mrs McGuire has been the senior nursing administrator here for several years, but she has gone on maternity leave,' she replied. 'There's a replacement taking over in September, but right now there's a bit of a staff crisis. Sister Barr on the women's ward will be acting administrator, and I'll take my turn at deputising for her.'

'Wow! Sounds as if you're to be a great big fish in a

very little pond, Jenny! Whatever made you give up a—?'

'Dr Forrest, I would be grateful if you will allow my theatre sister to give her full attention to her work. Thank you.'

Mr D'Arc's words were uttered in a tone of quiet command. He might have been asking for another type of suture, and did not even raise his head. The effect was instantaneous, and a silence followed in which the proverbial pin-drop could have been heard.

Steve Forrest mumbled an apology. 'Sorry, sir. Sister Curtis and I are—er...' He floundered to a stop, while Jenny blushed crimson with embarrassment. Even though the rebuke had been directed at Forrest, she felt herself included by the words 'my theatre sister'. What an idiotic prattler the consultant must think her, with no idea of theatre protocol or even basic good manners! She could have wept with vexation.

'Have you any T-25 dexon, Sister?' asked the consultant.

'Yes, sir.'

She fumbled in the suture tray, and a stitch-holder with a threaded needle attached slipped from her fingers and fell to the tiled floor with a clatter.

'*Damn!*' The word escaped before she could stop it. 'Oh, sorry!'

'All right, Sister, don't worry. Is there any more?' Mr d'Arc asked calmly.

'Yes, sir.' Doreen had whipped out another suture packet, torn it open and dropped the contents into the tray. Jenny attached it to another stitch-holder. 'Here, sir.'

'Three bags full, sir,' muttered Steve under his breath

as Mr d'Arc nodded and began to stitch the muscle layers with the same steady precision that he had shown from the start.

Not another word was spoken, and as soon as the last skin-clip had been inserted and Mrs Pritchard lifted from the table Jenny pulled off her gown and gloves and disappeared into the nearby ladies' cloakroom that served as a female changing-room. She splashed her burning cheeks with cold water, and grimaced at her reflection in the mirror. What a show-up in front of the theatre team!

But there was no time to brood over it for the instrument trolley had to be set ready for the next patient, a woman of twenty-eight.

'This poor girl has a large right ovarian cyst, beginning to show as an abdominal swelling,' said the consultant when Miss Royle lay before them on the table. 'Her mother suspected that she was pregnant, and a senior colleague at the library where she works persuaded her to go to her GP. She must have suffered great distress before the correct diagnosis was made.'

He carefully dissected out the melon-sized cyst. 'We can see that it was beginning to press upon other pelvic organs,' he observed. 'I have to decide whether to remove the whole ovary, leaving only the left one to function for her, or save it and risk a possible recurrence. Either way, her fertility will be decreased.'

The removed material was set aside in a large specimen jar for laboratory examination.

'I shall leave a small part of the ovary,' Mr d'Arc told them. 'Fortunately the cyst's encapsulated, and not likely to grow again. Still, if she were nearing the menopause I'd remove it. She'll need to be kept under review.'

By the time the operation was completed it was almost eleven o'clock, and traditionally time for a short break. Coffee and biscuits were brought from the hospital kitchen and served in an adjoining office where the theatre team relaxed in their blues, their caps, gowns and masks discarded.

'Come and sit down, Jenny, and let me pour you a nice strong cuppa,' invited Steve, taking charge of the coffee-pot. 'We've all earned one after the rarefied atmosphere in there. Oh, boy! Where's d'Arc gone? Not exactly comedian of the year, is he?'

'It's not his job to be, Steve,' retorted Jenny, picking up her cup. 'We behaved like a couple of silly kids in there.'

'Oh, don't take it to heart, love—remember how Charlie Steynes used to natter all the way through his lists? Said it helped him to concentrate,' responded the houseman cheerfully.

Dr McGuire looked up from his newspaper. 'I'll tell ye somethin', Dr Forrest—this man d'Arc's at the top o' his class. And Mr Steynes would've had your guts for shoelaces, so he would.'

Steve shrugged at Jenny. 'Well, it looks as if you'll be getting this top-class man for the next six months. Apparently he's been working in darkest Brazil for the last two years, all very primitive and other-worldly. He doesn't join in much of the social life at Bristol—and there are rumours of a mysterious woman in the background, so perhaps he—'

Jenny found herself unaccountably irritated, and put down her cup. 'How is your wife, Dr McGuire?' she asked abruptly.

The GP beamed in proud anticipation of fatherhood.

'She's pretty well, thanks, Sister Curtis, but a divil for not restin'. Thirty weeks she is now, and pinin' for this place, would ye believe it? Mind you, she always thought herself indispensable, that's her trouble.'

He laughed affectionately, and Jenny joined in a little wryly.

'She could be right, Dr McGuire. I feel that I've got an awful lot to learn about Stretbury Memorial.'

'Sure, and ye'd be welcome to call any time, Sister Curtis. The girl's in need of a continuous supply of hospital news. Ye'll be meetin' her at the antenatal clinic on Thursday, but mind ye keep her in her place!'

The rest of the list consisted of minor procedures—two diagnostic D and Cs, one of them including a cone biopsy, and a more extensive curettage for heavy, painful periods in a young mother. By half past twelve the list was complete, and Jenny could hardly wait to get into her sister's navy uniform dress and escape from the theatre.

'Coming for some lunch, Jenny?' Steve's voice called after her.

'No, thanks—I've got to look in at the Hylton annexe,' she replied over her shoulder.

A covered passageway led from the main hospital to the purpose-built single-storey annexe which housed the elderly residents, and into which Will Curtis had been admitted two weeks previously.

Sister Winnie Mason greeted Jenny with a sympathetic smile that did not quite conceal her frustration with Mr Curtis's lack of response.

'Not such a good day today, I'm afraid, Sister Curtis,' she said apologetically. 'The nurses met so much resistance to the toilet retraining programme that I took him over myself this morning, and tried to explain to him just *why* we want him to empty his bladder every hour. I've spent all the morning chatting with him and walking with him to the loo—and the only result is that he's no longer on speaking terms with me!'

'Did he *use* the loo, Sister Mason?' asked Jenny, her heart sinking.

'I'm afraid not, though we've had a couple of accidents,' sighed the middle-aged sister. 'He really is rather naughty, you know! I can't imagine how your poor grandmother coped when he started becoming incontinent.'

Jenny winced. She blamed herself bitterly for not noticing the deterioration in Grampy's behaviour, even though Grannie had done her best to hide it from her—until that dreadful day when she'd called unexpectedly at their overgrown cottage at Stretbury Green, and found Grannie in tears and Grampy aggressive. There was not a clean sheet in the cottage, and the unpleasant odour of stale urine pervaded every room.

'Why didn't you *tell* me, Grannie? Why did you go on struggling without any help?' Jenny had asked in horror.

'I didn't want to let Will down, Jenny. I've always looked up to him. He's been a good husband and I know he wouldn't want you or Dennis and Sheila to know how—how he's changed,' sobbed the exhausted old lady. 'Besides, I thought he might be taken away and put in one of those places with a lot of other old people—they just wouldn't understand him like I do. We've been married for nearly fifty years, Jenny, and shared the bad times as well as the good—we couldn't bear to be parted!'

Jenny's own tears had flowed at the sight of her grandmother's unhappiness, and she reproached herself for her
lack of observation.

She had at once contacted their GP, Dr Sellars, who'd
arranged for a domiciliary visit by a consultant in
Elderly Health Care, and Will Curtis had been whisked
off to a geriatric assessment unit in Bristol, from where
he had been transferred to the Hylton annexe, as a
Stretbury resident, for a course of rehabilitation and
treatment of incontinence. His wife was able to visit him
every day, but found his accusations of desertion hard
to bear.

Once alerted to the plight of the grandparents who had
brought her up, Jenny's conversations with Dr Sellars
and Sister Mason had led to an interview with the NHS
trust management committee of Stretbury Memorial
Hospital.

'You could be just the young lady we're looking for,
Miss Curtis,' beamed Lady Margaret Hylton, JP, the
founder's granddaughter and honorary chairman of the
committee.

'We urgently need a well-qualified nursing sister with
some theatre experience to take charge of our men's
ward and be able to deputise as Sister-in-charge until
our replacement for dear Sister McGuire is ready to take
up her post. You say you want to keep a close eye on
your grandparents so what could be simpler? This is
clearly one of those happy chances that brings the right
person to the right place at the right time!'

Which was why Jenny had given up an interesting
junior ward sister's post in a busy teaching hospital to
become 'a great big fish in a very little pond', as Steve
Forrest had so cheekily described her.

She had also given up the Bristol flat she had shared with two friends to move back into the cottage in which she had grown up. It was the only way that she could keep a proper check on her grandmother, and the old lady was deeply grateful for her company. For Jenny personally it was a backward step in every way, career-wise and socially. Stretbury was dull and quiet after life in the city, and she missed her many friendships there.

Well, what of it? she chided herself. Grannie and Grampy had virtually taken the place of parents, and after all they had given up for her since her inconvenient birth twenty-six years ago no sacrifice was too great to let them know how much she cared.

'Hallo, Grampy—it's me, Jenny.'

Two faded, anxious eyes stared up at her from under bushy brows, a permanent expression of worry in their depths.

'Jenny? Our little girl? Ah, Jenny!' His brow cleared momentarily. 'I *said* you'd come and take me home, didn't I? Yes, I told Doris you'd come, and she'll be wondering where I am so we'd better be going.'

Jenny took the gnarled hands in her own.

'Listen, Grampy, dear, you're in Stretbury Memorial Hospital where they're going to make you better—'

'There's nothing wrong with me!' he burst out crossly. 'How many times have I got to tell you? Oh, Jenny, don't *you* turn against me as well!'

His voice rose in agitation, and he looked so lost that Jenny's heart ached for him.

'All right, Grampy, all right—I know how you feel,' she said soothingly, sitting down beside him and holding his hands. After a minute or two the sound of her familiar voice had a calming effect, and he returned the pressure of her hand.

Sister Mason entered with two tablets in a plastic cup.

'Would you like to give him the one o'clock dose, Sister Curtis? It's his antidepressant and beta-blocker, both low doses. He may agree to accept them from *you*, otherwise we sometimes have long arguments about it!'

'Of course, Sister,' said Jenny at once. 'Now, Grampy, you're going to swallow these two little pills for me, aren't you? Good, I knew you would,' she said as he eyed them suspiciously. 'And then we'll both have one of these nice toffees—your favourites!'

A fair amount more coaxing was needed, but she eventually persuaded him to take the medication without being sidetracked into an argument. Afterwards she hugged him and unwillingly took her leave while he re-peated his pleas to be taken home.

Once out of the annexe, she took the garden path in preference to the covered passage, but had not gone more than two yards when a wave of dizziness seized her and she felt a stab of pain in her tummy. Was it time for her period already? She sat down heavily on one of the wooden bench seats beside the path. The green and gold of the daffodils blended and blurred before her eyes, and she realised to her dismay that she was crying.

'Grampy—oh, Grampy,' she whispered, remembering the father-figure she had always known and loved. She blinked hard, thankful that she was alone. It would never do to be caught sitting here in the hospital grounds and *bawling*, for heaven's sake!

And it was then that she felt the hand upon her shoulder, the strong, warm hand, comforting and calming. Of course—she had told Steve Forrest that she was going to call in at the annexe, and he had followed her. Good old Steve! Impulsively she covered his hand with her own in a grateful gesture.

'Sister Curtis…' began the deep voice, and Jenny started.

Merciful heavens, it wasn't Steve at all, but Mr d'Arc!

She gasped and snatched away her hand in confusion. When she raised her head slowly she found herself looking into two very deep blue eyes which were regarding her with concern. She had not really taken a proper look at the consultant in the theatre when he had worn a surgical mask and a theatre cap over his hair. This was the first opportunity she'd had to study his face, and she found herself quite taken by surprise.

With a complexion too warm to be described as olive and skin too smooth to be called swarthy, Findlay d'Arc nevertheless had a Latin look, matched by his thick, almost shaggy dark brown hair and heavy eyebrows. But there were reddish tints in the crisp curls, and the sea-blue eyes suggested a more northern influence, possibly Celtic—a fascinating combination.

His features were lean and aesthetic, with a network of fine little lines around his eyes and mouth, showing that time, experience and tropical suns had left their mark. There was something else—a sombreness, a shadow from the past that still persisted. He looked like a man who had known a great sorrow, Jenny thought, which made him sensitive to suffering in others.

'Sister Curtis, are you all right? Forgive me, but I followed you because I wanted to speak to you. Have you been visiting somebody in there?' He nodded towards the Hylton annexe.

Jenny realised that she had been staring, and recollected herself quickly.

'Mr d'Arc, I—I'm sorry,' she stammered, realising that the consultant must have been waiting for ten or fifteen minutes while she visited her grandfather.

He took a seat beside her on the bench. 'What is there to be sorry for, Sister? I only wanted to thank you for your competent assistance in the theatre this morning—not at all easy for you in new surroundings with an unknown surgeon. And I also want to make it absolutely clear that—'

He suddenly broke off. '*Is* anything the matter, Sister Curtis? I can see that you're upset about something.'

'I've just been visiting Grampy,' she heard herself confiding. 'My grandfather. He's seventy-nine now, and—well, he's beginning to lose touch with reality. Sister Mason and her staff are very good to the old people but, oh, it's so *undignifying* for him, having to walk to the toilet every hour—like a child learning to use a potty! Grampy was always very fastidious so— Oh, Mr d'Arc, he's been so strong and so wise, he and Grannie have made sacrifices for me, and—'

She pulled herself up sharply. What was she thinking of, telling all this to a virtual stranger? And yet it seemed so natural to pour out her heart to him…

She hesitated, looking up at him with troubled eyes.

'Oh, I'm sorry, Mr d'Arc, rattling on like this—you must think me a complete idiot!'

'It's all right, Sister. It sometimes helps to talk about these things,' he said thoughtfully. 'It's very sad when our loved ones become old and their minds cloud over, making them seem like different people. But that's when they need our love and care even more, and now it's your turn to repay what your grandfather did for you in the past.' He paused for a moment, then went on.

'Do I gather that this is the reason you have changed your job? I couldn't help overhearing what you said to Dr Forrest.'

'Oh, yes, and I'm sorry about that, too, Mr d'Arc— you must have thought—'

'Never mind about that, Sister, though, as a matter of fact, I wanted to apologise to you for any embarrassment over what I said to Dr Forrest. It was certainly not your fault. But have you really come to Stretbury Memorial because of your grandfather?'

'Yes, that's right, Mr d'Arc. And to keep an eye on Grannie. It's pretty awful for her, visiting him every day and being accused of having him locked up here!'

'But you have shown how much you care about them, Sister,' he pointed out. 'As a matter of fact, it is time that I checked up on my own elderly parents now that I've returned from South America.'

'Oh, do you mean Brazil?' asked Jenny, and then clapped her hand over her mouth like a guilty schoolgirl for revealing that he had been talked about during the coffee-break. His face lit up unexpectedly in a smile.

'I had forgotten the extraordinary speed of hospital gossip, Sister Curtis! Yes, it was in a remote part of Brazil, a little mission station in the middle of the jungle.'

'Oh, what was it like?' asked Jenny eagerly, unable to conceal her curiosity.

'Fairly primitive by NHS standards, but a good life. The hospital and clinic served an area of hundreds of square miles, and the work covered everything from

tropical diseases to some pretty makeshift obstetrics. I
learned a lot, and don't regret the time I spent there.'

'And were *you* a missionary, Mr d'Arc?' asked Jenny,
quite enthralled by this glimpse of such a different way
of life.

He laughed. 'Good heavens, no! I was employed by
them as an independent doctor and had my own bun-
galow. It was demanding at times, but good for me—it
stripped away the non-essentials and gave me a broader
perspective on things. I'd been drifting, and had reached
the end of my— But that's enough of all that.' He turned
and faced her.

'Feeling better now? I'd recommend you have some
lunch.'

She looked at her watch. 'Oh, no, it's a quarter past
one, and I'm back on duty at half past!'

'Then you'd better hurry, Sister.' She heard a hint of
amusement in his voice, and their eyes met in an unspoken exchange. After working in close co-ordination for
over three hours that morning, they seemed to have
learned quite a lot about each other in less than ten
minutes.

'Jenny!'

It was Steve Forrest calling as he strode towards them
across the lawn.

'Where on earth were you? I've looked all over—
Excuse me, Mr d'Arc, I thought you'd left an hour ago.'

'How strange, Dr Forrest, I thought that *you* had left.'

The consultant stood up as the houseman took Jenny's
arm. 'I must let you go, Sister Curtis. *Au revoir!*'

He nodded to them and retreated towards the car park.

'My word, you seem to have made a hit with our
friend Findlay,' observed Steve, steering her in the di-

rection of the main building. 'You must be starving, Jenny—let's see what's left on the hot plate!'

'I'll just have a sandwich and a coffee, Steve—I'm due to take over on the men's ward at one-thirty,' she told him.

'Then how about dinner this evening, Jenny? I could get over for half past eight, and take you to the Huntsman for a proper feed,' he urged, his fingers twining with hers.

'That's very kind of you, Steve, and I presume this means that it's all over between you and that little blonde staff nurse on A and E?' enquired Jenny pointedly.

'Oh, that was only to pass the time—on both sides,' he added quickly. 'As a matter of fact, Jenny, I'm a bit worried about you, stuck out here in the sticks, skipping meals, deputising here, there and everywhere. I'm going to keep an eye on you, my girl!'

He squeezed her arm, and Jenny smiled, delighted by his new-found interest in her since her move to Stretbury. She had thought him dishy on their first meeting a couple of months ago at Bristol, but he had scarcely noticed her—until now. She had only just begun her new job, but already felt her spirits rising. She was doing the right thing by her grandparents, and life at this little country hospital was certainly going to be varied, there was no doubt of that. Not to mention the Tuesday operating lists and working with the enigmatic Mr d'Arc...Stretbury Memorial might turn out to be not such a backwater after all!

CHAPTER TWO

JENNY had just finished the 2 p.m. observations and given out the four-hourly antibiotics.

'Right, gentlemen, time for a brew-up! And who wants one of my granny's delicious shortbread biscuits with his cuppa?'

At that moment Dr Graham Sellars strode into the men's ward.

'Hallo, young Jenny—I mean Sister Curtis. How are you finding life at Stretbury Memorial? Quite a change from a big teaching hospital, eh?'

He spoke with the easy familiarity of a middle-aged GP who had known her since childhood. As the senior partner in the practice and Vice-Chairman of the NHS trust committee for the hospital, he had used his influence with Lady Hylton to recommend Jenny for her present post.

'I've just looked in at the Hylton annexe to see your grandfather,' he went on. 'Still having quite a few problems, isn't he?'

'If you mean that he's driving Sister Mason and her staff round the bend—well, yes, Dr Sellars,' she answered wryly.

'These antidepressants that he's on can take three or four weeks to show any effect,' said Sellars. 'And we must be realistic, you know. There's no miracle cure for old age, my dear.'

He spoke kindly, but Jenny was discovering how difficult it was to be sensible and accept the inevitable when the patient was someone close and dear. She was silent.

'Anyway, I've got a couple of investigations coming up for Thursday morning,' he said. 'Let's go into the office, and I'll tell you about them.'

The nursing auxiliary on duty went to put the kettle on—almost a reflex action, Jenny noticed, when a doctor appeared on the ward.

'The one that will concern you is Mr Peter Gould, Headmaster of Stretbury Junior and Primary School,' said Dr Sellars. 'Mr Jamieson wants to do a colonoscopy and biopsy. The other's an old lady for cystoscopy, a friend of Lady Hylton. She'll be a day case.'

'What—*here*, Dr Sellars?' asked Jenny, thinking of the extensive facilities at her former hospital where consultant surgeon Mr Jamieson practised.

'Yes, he'll bring his 'scopes with him, and use the theatre. Mr Gould will have to be on fluids only for twenty-four hours, and have a high colonic wash-out on Thursday morning, so he'll be admitted tomorrow evening. He knows quite a few of the staff here who have children at his school.'

'Poor man! How embarrassing for him to be among people who look up to him as their children's headmaster!' Jenny's lively features became serious.

'My dear girl, he's getting preferential treatment on the NHS! He and the old lady won't have to make a thirty-mile round trip to Mr Jamieson's clinic just because they're who they are.'

Jenny shrugged. 'Maybe so, but I think I'd rather be among strangers if somebody was gazing up my bottom through a tube with a torch on the end—wouldn't *you*, Dr Sellars?'

Before the astonished GP could work out an answer to this interesting thought they were joined by Sister Louise Barr, an attractive, fair-haired woman in her mid-thirties who was in charge of the women's ward at Stretbury Memorial. She had come to ask Jenny to check post-operative injections of morphine for Mrs Pritchard and Miss Royle.

'Oh, me, oh, my!' she said with a smile. 'I got a glimpse of Mr Tall, *d'Arc* and Handsome in the theatre this morning—wow! What's he like to scrub up for?'

'Fantastic—knows his job, works at a steady pace, keeps his cool and seems a very caring man,' answered Jenny promptly.

'Oho! He's obviously made a big impression on our new sister, hasn't he, Dr Sellars?' Louise accompanied the words with a knowing wink that irritated Jenny. 'And he'll be back on Thursday afternoon for the antenatal clinic.'

'Why should a consultant obstetrician come all this way to a six-bed maternity unit?' asked Jenny in surprise. 'There can't be that many antenatal mums to see.'

'My dear Jenny, there'll be at least forty!' laughed Dr Sellars. 'Mr d'Arc's predecessor, Mr Steynes, used to see *all* his antenatals in this catchment area, not just the happy few booked for delivery here. It saves them a lot of travelling, especially those with young children. I hope this Mr d'Arc will be willing to carry on the tradition—there'll be trouble if he doesn't!'

Jenny found herself hoping so too, and then immediately wondered why on earth it should make any difference to her.

'Dennis has been on the phone, Jenny,' said her grandmother when she arrived at Bailey's Cottage soon after

five and put her bicycle away in Grampy's tool-shed.
Would he ever use it again? she wondered sadly, looking
at the neat rows of garden implements.

'What did Dennis say, Grannie?'

'Well, he asked about Will, of course, and said he'd
try to get up this weekend.'

'Will Sheila and the children be coming too?' asked
Jenny, with mixed feelings at the thought of such an
invasion.

'No, dear, he'll come on his own and get some jobs
done around the house, he said.'

'Great!' replied Jenny with relief. 'Those shrubs need
cutting back in the front garden, and so does the privet
hedge. I should have tackled them long ago,' she added
guiltily, thinking of Grannie's lonely struggle through
the winter as her husband's health had deteriorated, with
consequent neglect of the cottage. Jenny hoped for an
opportunity to have a heart-to-heart talk with Dennis
about the future of the old couple who were his parents
and her grandparents.

'Have you had a good day, Grannie? Wait till I tell
you about mine! And, guess what, I'm being taken out
to dinner this evening! Don't worry, I won't be late
back,' she added quickly, seeing the old lady's worried
look. 'Is the kettle on? I could murder for a cup of tea,
couldn't you?'

Jenny was adding the finishing touches to her make-up
when Steve's car drew up outside. She had put on a
Paisley-patterned dress with a white collar, and her navy
wool jacket was thrown over a chair. It was smarter than

the comfortable black leather jacket she wore to cycle to the hospital.

'The—er—the young man's here, dear!' Grannie called up the stairs.

'Yes, Grannie, I'm just coming—won't be a minute!'

Squinting in the ancient triple mirror, mascara brush in hand, she blinked suddenly and a blob landed under her eye.

'Oh, I've gone and smudged it—damn!'

She rushed to the bathroom, but her attempts to wash away the mistake only spread the blob and she had to start all over again. She heard Grannie's voice in the hall, offering Steve a cup of tea, which he politely declined.

How different from the easy informality of the Bristol flat she had shared with friends who were always coming and going! Steve would have sprawled on the huge, squashy settee and chatted with whoever was around while Jenny got ready to go out, and the accident with the mascara would have been a joke.

Poor Grannie clearly suspected the good-looking doctor of pursuing her granddaughter with intentions that might or might not be honourable. The memory of Jenny's mother's experience made her nervous when men showed any interest in the pretty, high-spirited girl, and it was one reason why Jenny had been thankful to escape to the freedom of Bristol where boyfriends did not have to be interrogated when they called.

She now hurried downstairs and found Steve talking to Mrs Curtis about the cottage, and hearing that it was over two hundred years old, having been built for the farm bailiff of the Lord Hylton of that time. The young doctor was impressed.

'You could make a bomb by selling this to some professional couple who'd do it up and put in a few mod cons, Jenny! It's a nice little property, and basically substantial. Wouldn't mind something like it myself when I'm ready to settle down with a nice wife and two point four children!'

Jenny was surprised, as she had never looked on Bailey's Cottage as having real value. On the contrary, she only saw a rather inconvenient, old-fashioned house hemmed in by a rampaging garden. Yet it was her home, and she would be living in it for the foreseeable future, as long as her grandparents needed her.

She tried to relax as they drove towards the A38, and the Huntsman, five miles north of Stretbury. Of course it was flattering to be escorted by a man like Steve to a good restaurant, which had once been a coaching inn on the Gloucester Road. He ordered steak and a bottle of red wine with the meal. Jenny settled for garlic mushrooms with a side salad, but found that she had very little appetite when it arrived. They chose ice cream for dessert, and Steve persuaded her to have a Gaelic coffee while he drank black as he was driving.

It should have been an enjoyable evening with a hint of romance in the spring air, and Jenny was quite cross with herself for feeling both tired and tense. The only effect of the alcohol was to give her a headache. In spite of Steve's attentiveness and light-hearted anecdotes, she could not conceal a yawn and apologised shamefacedly.

'Sorry, Steve—it's nothing to do with you, honestly. It's just that I've got a lot on my mind right now—and such heaps to learn about Stretbury Memorial. Look, it's nearly half past ten—perhaps you'd better take me home now. I'm not very jolly company, am I?'

He was all concern for her. 'I say, Jenny, don't let them take advantage of you at that little one-horse place—it's no life for a girl like you! When shall I see you again? How are you fixed for the weekend?'

'On call.'

'What about next Monday? I could get here for seven-thirty.'

'Oh, Steve, you must be a glutton for punishment! Actually, I think I shall quite enjoy the job when I get settled—I might as well, seeing that I've no choice, really.'

She could have added that her worries over her grandparents and her new responsibilities at the little country hospital seemed to leave no time for any emotional entanglements, at least for the time being.

When they reached Bailey's Cottage Jenny thanked him for a pleasant evening, pecked him lightly on the cheek, wriggled free of his eager arms and leapt nimbly out of the passenger door. He saw her disappear behind the darkly looming privet hedge without a backward glance.

Young Dr Forrest looked thoughtful: clearly, Sister Curtis was no pushover.

Even before she reached the hospital on Thursday morning Jenny felt that it was going to be one of those days...

'Will you be OK to help out in the antenatal clinic this afternoon, Sister Curtis?' asked Wendy Garrett, the midwife in charge of the little maternity ward. 'We need all hands on deck when the number 157 bus arrives at half past two with a whole lot of mothers from Wotton and the other side of the M5.'

'I'll do my best, Sister, but I've got a patient for

colonoscopy this morning. I'll have to assist in Theatre for that and a cystoscopy, too. It won't leave much time to give to the rest of my patients, poor chaps.'

'Oh, but they're all straightforward post-ops, over the worst by the time you get them,' answered Wendy, dismissing her objection. 'Sister McGuire always used to set aside Thursday afternoons to help out with the clinic.'

Jenny was getting just a little tired of hearing about Mrs McGuire's indispensability.

'I'll do my best, Sister, only I'm a bit worried about my Mr Gould and shall stay with him until it's all over— OK? I should be free by the time the Expectant Express pulls in!'

Peter Gould was a scholarly man of fifty-seven, and had been headmaster of the Stretbury school for over ten years. Jenny felt that he needed counselling, but had no idea whom she could ask to see him. Her friendly overtures and explanations of what was involved in the procedure had met with politeness but also a certain defensiveness on his part.

He even addressed his worried wife in carefully matter-of-fact tones, avoiding any show of affection. He told her not to get into a state, that the whole business would soon be over and then he could get back to dealing with the day-to-day pressures of running a school.

Jenny had smiled and nodded, but was not deceived. She saw the fear in his eyes, the dread of the coming examination and of what it could reveal. And of what might follow.

She accompanied him to the theatre at ten, having given him a sedative injection ordered by the surgeon.

'Don't worry, this will send you floating away on a little fluffy cloud, Mr Gould,' she had told him brightly. 'After ten minutes you won't care if it snows, I promise!'

The examination was over within half an hour, and after he had been returned to the ward Jenny was a little taken aback to find the impressive figure of Lady Margaret Hylton waiting for her in the entrance hall, wearing a flowing green cloak over her two-piece suit and sporting a feathered hat.

'My dear Sister Curtis, how is that poor man? His staff are terribly worried—so many rumours going round, as usual! Isn't it good of Mr Jamieson to do these investigations here? My poor friend, Agnes, is having a general anaesthetic for hers so I'll wait until she's round.'

Jenny smiled politely, hoping she would not be detained long, but her ladyship's next words almost bowled her over.

'Anyway, Sister, dear, I want you to come to a little dinner party at my home next Monday evening, if that's convenient for you. I do like to get to know new members of the staff, and there's nothing like a good meal to provide just the right atmosphere, don't you agree?'

'Er—why, yes, Lady Hylton, thank you very much,' answered Jenny in some confusion.

'Splendid! I'll expect you at about eight, then. Have you got transport?'

Good heavens, thought Jenny, I can't wear a decent outfit to *cycle* up to Stretbury Manor! Aloud, she stammered, 'I don't actually drive, but I can order a—'

'Oh, I'm sure Mr d'Arc will be able to call for you and bring you with him,' beamed her ladyship. 'I'll have a word with him. It's Stretbury Green, isn't it—Bailey's Cottage?'

Jenny swallowed. 'Yes, but, honestly, Lady Hylton, there's no need to bother Mr d'Arc—'

'Who's bothering me?' asked a deep voice as the figure of the consultant came through the front entrance, casually dressed in a tweed jacket with brown corduroys. 'Good morning, Sister Curtis and Mrs…er…'

His tone was direct and friendly, but Jenny had to suppress a grin at his failure to recognise the formidable lady, who was quite unoffended.

'Good heavens, you must be Mr Findlay d'Arc!' she exclaimed. 'We spoke on the telephone last night, and arranged for you to come to dinner next Monday, if you remember.'

'Lady Hylton, I do apologise! Delighted to meet you in person,' he said, swiftly holding out his hand.

'I was just telling Sister Curtis that you will be able to give her a lift, Mr d'Arc.'

Jenny squirmed with embarrassment, but he assured her of his willingness to act as chauffeur, and she could only mutter her thanks.

'I know I'm early for the clinic,' he went on, 'but I'd like to see the ladies who had ops on Tuesday, and then I'll take a more leisurely look at this hospital, seeing that I'll have quite a close connection with it. I might as well get its measure!'

Lady Hylton was enchanted. 'I shall have the greatest pleasure in taking you on a tour, Mr d'Arc. I pride myself on the high standards here—you'll find the nursing care second to none!'

Jenny chuckled to herself as she returned to the theatre for the cystoscopy. Whatever would she think of to say at a dinner party? She presumed that Mr d'Arc was invited for the same reason as herself, a newcomer to be sussed out. What an absolute scream! Her friends at Bristol would laugh their heads off to see her hobnobbing with ladyships and consultants at Maison de Posh!

When she returned to the men's ward she found that Lady Hylton had preceded her; Mr d'Arc's attention was being drawn to the various amenities. He nodded and looked suitably impressed, stopping to have a word with every patient.

Jenny remembered Mr Gould, recovering from his ordeal in the one single cubicle that the ward possessed.

'Oh, excuse me. Lady Hylton, don't go in there, please!' she said quickly. 'It's essential that Mr Gould is left undisturbed, if you don't mind.'

Lady Hylton looked surprised, but said she must defer to Sister Curtis's wishes. An idea came to Jenny in a flash of inspiration.

'Actually, your friend will be coming round from her anaesthetic, Lady Hylton, and she'll be wanting you beside her,' she said artfully. 'Mr d'Arc seems to be quite happy, chatting to the men, doesn't he?'

'Thank you, Sister, dear. I'll go to poor Agnes at once.'

She swept out of the ward and Jenny sighed thankfully, then she discreetly approached Mr d'Arc and asked him if he would come into the office for a moment. He came at once, a concerned expression in his eyes.

'I couldn't help overhearing you, Sister, when you spoke of this—er—Mr Gould, is it? May I ask what his problem is?'

'Oh, you've taken the words right out of my mouth, sir!' she said gratefully, pointing him to a chair beside the desk. 'He's headmaster of the local school and—

well, he may have lower bowel cancer. Mr Jamieson didn't look very happy with what the colonoscopy showed this morning. A biopsy was taken, and when the lab report comes back he'll know for sure.'

Mr d'Arc's strangely blue eyes never left her face as he sat at the desk, his long hands lightly clasped together.

'Has Mr Gould said anything of his feelings to you, Sister Curtis? About the possibility of surgery?'

'No. I don't think he's even spoken to his wife, though the poor woman's worried sick.' She pushed the casenotes towards him. 'It was she who insisted that he went to his GP when she found that he'd been passing blood in the toilet. He was given an urgent appointment with Mr Jamieson, and here we are. If it's cancer of the colon he'll be for major surgery and a colostomy, won't he?'

The consultant nodded. 'Yes, and an intelligent man such as he knows this as well as you or I, Sister. And he must be just as anxious as we would be.'

Jenny drew a deep breath. 'Mr d'Arc, he's terrified and needs to talk to somebody. Only who do you ask to counsel a man like that, for heaven's sake? I'd ask the vicar from the parish church—he's very nice and understanding—but it might not be very tactful, and I don't know how Mr Gould would react. What do you think?'

Mr d'Arc nodded slowly. 'I see what you mean, Sister. You don't want to offer something that he has not asked for. He's probably clinging desperately to his pride, poor chap!'

'So what I'm asking you, Mr d'Arc, seeing that you're an understanding man and fellow professional…'

'Ah! You want me to speak to him, Sister.'

'*Would* you?' she pleaded.

'But, as we've already said, he may not wish it, Sister.' His voice was serious, but Jenny was determined to persist.

'Forgive me, Mr d'Arc, but you look as if you've had some experience with this sort of thing.'

He turned his head sharply to face her, and she saw a very dark shadow lurking in the deep blue eyes.

'You could say that, Sister, yes.' He got up. 'Very well, I'll go and introduce myself. What's his first name?'

'Peter. Thanks a million, sir.'

She followed him to the door of the single room, and heard his opening words.

'Hallo, there—you're Peter Gould, aren't you? Findlay's the name, and I'm having a look round the hospital. By the way, I'm into gynaecology so no need for alarm! I believe they've given you one hell of a time this morning, old chap—'

The door was closed, and Jenny heard no more. Three quarters of an hour passed, and she eventually called Findlay to come for lunch before his clinic began. He looked very thoughtful when he emerged, but gave Jenny a thumbs-up sign.

'How is he?' she asked. 'Was it very difficult?'

He did not reply directly. 'I think a cup of tea would be well received, Sister, and maybe a bite of something—only please take it to him yourself, don't send your staff nurse. He knows her as a parent, and he's not up to that kind of socialising yet. He'd like to see his wife, though.'

'Great! I'll call her right away. I'm afraid this has taken up a lot of your time, sir,' she added guiltily.

'Don't worry, Sister, I'm glad you asked me.'

As he hurried away Jenny noticed that her staff nurse and auxiliary stared after him, their eyes wide with curiosity and admiration in about equal measure.

'Who was *that*, Sister?'

She avoided their questions, perhaps because her own thoughts about this man were so strangely unsettling. When she took tea and toast to Peter Gould she found him sitting up, his library book open on the bed. He quickly wiped his eyes with a tissue from a box on the locker.

'Sister, who was that doctor?' he asked.

'Mr Findlay d'Arc, the new obs and gynae man—he's taken over Mr Steynes's consultancy at Bristol,' she answered, smiling.

'But why did he come to see *me* just now?'

Jenny decided that truth was the safest option.

'I asked him to, Mr Gould. I felt that you needed to talk about things,' she said quietly.

'But, Sister, how did you *know*?' he asked in bewilderment. 'I gave you no indication. I kept my thoughts entirely to myself—I'm used to doing so. In fact, I actually told you that I didn't need to discuss this—er—investigation. Even Brenda, my wife, had no idea of how I—'

Jenny's brown eyes met his directly. 'I know, I know, but there are some things that can't be hidden, Mr Gould. Don't forget that nurses have some experience of patients' reactions! You wouldn't be human if you didn't feel a bit alarmed at what's happened to you out of the blue—would you?'

'Alarmed? Oh, Sister Curtis! Alarm—fear—disgust and revulsion at the thought of my body being mutilated. The very idea of having to cope with one of those—

bags. In fact, I'd come to the conclusion that I'd rather die.'

He paused for a moment, then cleared his throat and went on, 'I felt such a coward, so utterly alone. My self-esteem had never been at a lower ebb—until today. But now I've been able to tell somebody, and everything's different. I opened my eyes, and there was this man, Findlay, whom I've never seen before in my life, standing there and talking to me. And he knew all about it. I'm absolutely convinced that he was sent to me in my worst hour.

'And I feel better now, stronger, able to face whatever has to be. Oh, Sister! I'm so grateful!'

His voice broke, and Jenny put her hand on his shoulder.

'All right, Mr Gould—Peter—it's OK,' she said softly, and felt her own eyes misting as he looked up and smiled at her through tears, no longer ashamed of his emotion. Whatever might happen to Peter Gould's body, the man himself was restored to wholeness again. And was perhaps a little wiser than he had been before, thanks to the intervention of Findlay d'Arc.

The hospital boardroom did duty as an antenatal clinic, as Jenny soon discovered. Posters adorned the walls, proclaiming the merits of healthy eating, the joys of breast-feeding and the evils of smoking. The big mahogany table was spread with information leaflets, covering everything from maternity benefits to dentistry and social services in the area.

One corner of the room was sectioned off for young children to play with building bricks, simple wooden jigsaws and other toys, while in the opposite corner was a

screened alcove behind which Miss Garrett had an examination couch and saw her own booked patients.

'Whoops! Steady on there, young man,' said Jenny,
bending over and scooping up a little boy of about a
year old who was speeding on all fours towards Miss
Garrett's corner. She held him up aloft to the company.

'Does this belong to anybody, or shall I send it to
Lost Property?'

There was a ripple of laughter as an apologetic young
mother claimed her firstborn. Jenny was about to start
chatting to her when the midwife emerged from her lair,
foetal stethoscope in hand.

'I believe you're a registered midwife, Sister Curtis?'

'Yes, but I went back to general nursing after a year,'
replied Jenny.

'Right, then you won't be much use at interviewing
and advising. My staff nurse does the weighing, blood
pressures and urine testing so you'd better chaperon the
consultant this afternoon—he's just gone into his room
over there, next to the board room. There's a little office
beside it where I shall send the mothers through to be
seen. Make sure all the case-cards are filled in, and send
each mother back to me when he's seen her—all right?'

'Great! I like to feel useful and needed,' murmured
Jenny, winking at the little boy's mother.

Mr d'Arc greeted his assistant with his slow smile.
'You seem to be everywhere, Sister Curtis. Who's looking after the men's ward this afternoon?'

'Staff Nurse Barnett. I've warned her not to gossip to
Mr Gould about school matters, by the way. He's just
so grateful to you, Mr d'Arc—and so am I.'

'Let me know how he goes on, Sister. I think he'll be

one of your transferred post-op patients fairly soon,' he said gravely. 'Now, are there some ladies for me to see?'

There was a steady stream of ladies over the next two hours, from late teenage to nearly forty-one years—married, divorced and remarried, and single with or without stable relationships. The consultant approached each one of them with the same formal courtesy, calling them all 'Mrs'—just as he addressed Jenny as Sister Curtis, in contrast to the current fashion for first names.

When a fresh-faced woman in her mid-thirties with neatly bobbed hair bustled in and climbed onto the couch with an experienced air, Jenny sensed the arrival of a VIP.

'Good afternoon, Mr d'Arc—and you, too, Sister Curtis,' said the lady briskly. 'How relieved I was to hear of your appointment! I've been so conscience-stricken about leaving Stretbury Memorial in the lurch. In fact, I haven't been able to sleep for worrying about it.'

Findlay glanced at the case-card. 'Ah, hello, Mrs McGuire,' he said with a smile, while Jenny mumbled her response. 'I note that everything seems to be fine—blood pressure OK, urine clear, weight sixty-seven kilograms. You're due on June 27th, so that makes you...' he consulted his obstetric calendar '...just over thirty weeks. Good!'

'I've worked out that I'm due around June 20th, but time will show,' said the expectant mother confidently. 'Are you going to send me for a scan at thirty-two weeks, Mr d'Arc?'

'For what reason, Mrs McGuire?'

'It was Mr Steynes's routine with his—'

'But Mr Steynes is no longer here, my dear. You seem

perfectly normal in every way. The fundal height corresponds with your dates, the foetal heart is strong and regular. Is your baby moving around? Well done! Are you taking your iron? Good! Come and see me in another three weeks unless you have any problems.'

Mrs McGuire raised her eyebrows. 'Very well, Mr d'Arc.'

She hopped off the couch without his assistance, and turned to Jenny.

'So pleased to meet you, Sister Curtis, and remember that you have only to call me on the phone if you have any problems here at SMH. Conor speaks very highly of you! I'll be in touch—and do call me Anne.'

Jenny murmured politely, 'Nice to have met you—er—Anne. Will you—er—see Miss Garrett before you leave, please?'

'Don't worry, I know the drill. Good afternoon!'

Seizing her case-card, Anne McGuire swished out of the room, her voluminous maternity dress flicking up at the hem.

'A sensible, forthright girl,' remarked Findlay. 'It will be a pleasure to look after her when she has her baby.'

Jenny coughed discreetly. She could hardly imagine anything worse than having the legendary Sister McGuire breathing down her neck. Or having to care for her in the maternity ward.

'Yes, very nice, sir. Is she—er—booked for delivery here?' Jenny tried to sound casual as she changed the paper sheet on the examination couch.

He shook his head. 'Oh, no. I don't like having primigravidas in isolated GP units with limited facilities, especially if they're doctors' wives! I shall probably admit her at thirty-nine weeks for assessment.'

As Jenny turned to open the door and call in the next patient she felt his eyes upon her, and turned round to face him. The twinkle in his deep blue eyes caught her off guard.

'So you can breathe again, Sister Curtis!'

The man's a mind-reader, she thought, but her wary smile broadened into a grin.

'Honestly, Mr d'Arc, I think she's really nice—otherwise Dr McGuire wouldn't have married her, would he?'

He shook his head slowly. 'Ah, Sister Curtis, one never can tell with other people's marriages, but I think I understand what you mean. Conor adores her. She's carrying his child and that makes him a very happy man. Lucky Dr McGuire!'

Jenny stared in frank astonishment at this unexpected remark from a man who had apparently turned his back on civilisation and what had clearly been a successful career to work in a remote part of the Third World. Steve Forrest had said something about a woman. Was it because of a woman that he had gone away? she wondered. And why had he now returned to a world where women like Louise Barr and Staff Nurse Barnett openly admired his looks and manners?

'All right, Sister, send in the next lady, please.'

She hastily recollected herself.

'Oh, yes, of course, Mr d'Arc—sorry!'

As he stood beside the couch and gently palpated the tummy of the mother lying there Jenny found herself staring at the back of his dark head, and remembered how patiently he had listened when she'd told him about

Grampy. And how he had transformed Peter Gould's dread into hope and courage.

No doubt about it—Mr d'Arc was somebody really special, whatever Steve Forrest thought about him.

CHAPTER THREE

DENNIS CURTIS arrived at the cottage on Friday evening, having driven up from his home in Somerset.

'I can stay till Sunday evening,' he told his mother and Jenny. 'That'll give me time to tidy up the garden, and I've got a pal in Stretbury who'll give me a hand with those loose floorboards and the leak in the cistern.'

Taking Jenny aside, he reproached her for not sending for him earlier. 'For heaven's sake, Jen, why didn't you let us *know* you were having trouble with Dad?'

Jenny sighed and bit her lip. It was hard to explain that Grannie had kept her equally in the dark, although she felt that she had less excuse for ignorance, living so much closer to her grandparents. Dennis saw her discomfiture and remembered that she had given up a good post in Bristol to come home to keep an eye on Grannie.

'I appreciate what you're doing, Jen,' he conceded, 'and so does Sheila. I know it puts the main burden on you, with us living so far away.'

'It's all right, I owe it to them,' she said quickly. 'And I think I'll enjoy my new job when I get used to it.'

'Can you take time off the weekend after next?' he went on. 'It's our Amanda's eleventh birthday, and Sheila's giving her a special party for passing her eleven-plus. She'd really like you and Mum to be there. I know Dad can't make it, but I hope you can persuade Mum.'

Old Mrs Curtis's face creased in her usual worried frown on hearing of the invitation.

'I couldn't leave Will for a whole weekend, son. He looks out for me to visit him every day—and it's such a long way from here to Dewsfold.'

'Don't worry, Mum, I'll come and fetch you and Jen, and bring you back again,' said Dennis, turning to Jenny who was eager to accept.

'Yes, I'm off that weekend, fortunately, but it's a dickens of a drive for you, Dennis—two journeys each way.'

'Easy! Straight up the A358 to Taunton, and then onto the M5. I can do it in under two hours,' he assured her.

'We *must* be there to congratulate Amanda, Grannie,' urged Jenny, who felt that they should accept the invitation from Dennis's wife. Besides, she felt that her grandmother needed a break from Will's daily accusations of betrayal.

'Good, that's settled, then,' said Dennis. 'Sheila will be really pleased, and the kids'll be over the moon!'

When they went to visit Grampy on the Saturday he thought his son had come to take him home, and his disappointment was distressing to them all. Jenny had a word with the sister about the possibility of taking him home for a few hours, but Winnie Mason considered it too early to try out a home visit.

'And, besides, he hasn't really improved so far with the toilet training,' she pointed out. 'I honestly think it would be better to wait another week or two, and use the promise of a home visit as a reward for good progress. It will be an incentive for him.'

However, Dennis was unable to withstand his father's pleas, and said he would accept responsibility for taking him home for a few hours, returning after tea. Will was accordingly dressed in his outdoor clothes and shoes, and Dennis led him out to the car while Jenny followed with a bundle of incontinence pads and plastic sheets to spread over chairs and car seats. She then had to go on duty for the afternoon shift.

As Winnie had predicted, it was not a success, and when Will was unwillingly returned to the Hylton annexe at six Jenny was called over from the men's ward to try to reason with him and to comfort Grannie, who was in tears. Dennis was now convinced that his father would have to become a permanent resident there.

'Dad followed me around all the time, Jen, so I haven't got all the jobs done that I'd planned,' he apologised glumly, and Jenny hadn't the heart to retort that he should have taken the sister's advice.

After Dennis had left them, Jenny's mind turned to the approaching dinner party at Stretbury Manor and how to prepare Grannie for another gentleman caller at Bailey's Cottage.

'He's a consultant, Grannie, and quite old, really,' she said airily. 'We've both been invited to dinner with Lady Hylton, and she asked him to pick me up—I mean, call for me at seven-thirty.'

'But what about the other young man, Jenny?' asked the old lady. 'He seemed to think a lot of you. What will *he* say about this other doctor taking you out?'

Her tone was a mite disapproving, and Jenny had to remind herself to be patient with Grannie's constant fears. She laughed a little self-consciously.

'Steve? Oh, he's just a friend, Grannie, nothing serious. And he doesn't even know about Mr d'Arc giving me a lift so what does it matter?'

She was soon to find out.

When she had finished dressing and was studying her reflection in the old triple mirror she heard the sound of a car engine, and was horrorstruck to see two cars drawing up outside the newly clipped hedge. Both drivers got out and looked at each other in surprise.

'Good evening, Dr Forrest.'

'Er—hello, Mr d'Arc.'

'Good heavens!' whispered Jenny incredulously, looking down from the window. 'Oh, *no*!'

Standing back out of sight, she saw Findlay lead the way to the front door and raise the horseshoe knocker. Steve stood behind him, a distinctly puzzled expression on his handsome face. When Doris Curtis opened the door Findlay smiled down at her and held out his hand.

'Mrs Curtis? Good evening! I'm Findlay d'Arc, and I've come to call for your granddaughter to take her to Stretbury Manor. Is she ready yet?'

Doris stared uncertainly up into the kind blue eyes of the tall man, and her features relaxed.

'Oh, yes, Dr—er—Findlay, she's expecting you. Would you like to come in and wait for her?'

Findlay thanked her and walked over the threshold into a hallway from which a flight of stairs ran up to the first floor. Doris showed him into a low-ceilinged parlour.

'And good evening from me too, Mrs Curtis,' said Steve, raising his voice a little. 'I've arranged to take Jenny out to dinner, but it seems that I have some competition.'

Mrs Curtis peered at him in the dim passage. 'I'm

sorry, Doctor, but she's not expecting *you*,' she said bluntly. 'Only Dr Findlay.'

'Well, I'll wait and see her, if you don't mind,' said Steve, coming in and following Findlay into the parlour, where they eyed each other somewhat warily—though Findlay remarked conversationally that it was a fine evening.

Jenny slowly descended the stairs in a short black tailored skirt, crisp white blouse and new red jacket.

'I know, Grannie, I *know*,' she muttered as Mrs Curtis pointed towards the parlour. 'I completely forgot that Steve was coming over. I thought he said Tuesday, like last week.'

'Well, I hope you stay with that Dr Findlay—he's got the kind of face I trust to do right,' declared the old lady.

'*Shh*, Grannie, they'll hear you!' hissed Jenny, rolling her eyes heavenwards and putting a finger to her lips. 'I shall have to go in there and apologise. This has to be the worst nightmare I was ever in!'

Holding her head up and her shoulders back, she approached the parlour with the air of a martyr going to the block.

'Good evening, Mr d'Arc—and Steve,' she said bravely. 'Can I say how sorry I am for this mess—I mean, this ghastly mistake?'

'I distinctly said Monday this week, Jenny, when we left the Huntsman last Tuesday,' Steve reminded her, emphasising that their arrangement predated any that Findlay might have made.

'And I am merely here to offer you a lift, Miss Curtis,' said Findlay tactfully. 'We are both invited to dinner with Lady Hylton and, if you still want to go, my offer still stands.'

'Of *course* I still want to go!' Jenny was ready to die of embarrassment. 'Look, Steve, I'm just so sorry. I can't think how I forgot about this evening—I mean, I was sure it was tomorrow. I'm afraid I'm committed to this dinner party at Stretbury Manor. I'm *sorry*, Steve, I really am.'

She gestured helplessly, but Steve's voice was tight.

'So you're going to this old girl's bash, Jenny, in preference to a new Thai restaurant in Bristol where I've booked a table for two?'

Findlay strolled over to the window, apparently to admire the view, while Jenny repeated her apologies to Steve but insisted that Lady Hylton's dinner party took priority.

'I mean, it's part of my job, really,' she pleaded, running a hand distractedly through her short brown hair until it stood wildly up on end. 'Steve, I'm just so *sorry*.'

Findlay turned round. 'It is most unfortunate, Dr Forrest, but these hitches do happen,' he said pleasantly. 'So, if you'll excuse us, we'd better be going.' He looked at his watch. 'I believe Lady Hylton said that dinner was at eight, didn't she, Miss Curtis?'

Steve made a determined effort to hide his annoyance, deciding that gracious good humour was his best option.

'All right, Jenny, darling, I understand. Don't worry about it. I'll call you tomorrow, right? We'll arrange something else soon. Have a jolly time with her ladyship!'

Stepping towards her he gave her a quick kiss on the lips, and with a smiling farewell to her grandmother he turned on his heel and left.

'Good, that means you won't have to say ''sorry'' any

more,' said Findlay, and Jenny was not sure whether he was sympathetic or trying to suppress his amusement.

'Phew! My first thought was to climb out of the window, shin down a drainpipe and run for it!' She giggled nervously.

'Right, are we ready to go?' he asked. 'Goodnight, Mrs Curtis, and I'm very pleased to have met you!'

He took Grannie's hand in his, and she smiled up at him happily. 'Goodnight, Dr Findlay, and I'm so glad that Jenny chose you!' she told him.

Her granddaughter winced and avoided Findlay's eye as he opened the passenger door for her. The shortness of her black skirt made her feel distinctly leggy as she got in and she wished she'd chosen another longer style, but it was too late now.

He hasn't said anything about how I look, she thought, but perhaps he doesn't notice things like women's clothes. He was conventionally dressed in a dark grey suit with a white shirt and university tie.

A faint but deliciously spicy tang wafted towards her as he fastened his seat belt, and Jenny thought she recognised a world-famous and expensive French soap. It surprised her to think that such an unworldly man would indulge himself in that kind of luxury, but perhaps somebody had given it to him as a present.

'I like your grandmother,' he said as they pulled out of Stretbury Green.

'And you've certainly made a hit with *her*, Mr d'Arc! She's usually terribly suspicious of anything male that comes calling,' answered Jenny wryly.

'Yes, I got the impression that she's very protective of you, Jenny!'

Jenny! His use of her first name gave her an odd little

frisson of pleasure, knowing his usual formality. Should she reciprocate and call him Findlay? She had never yet called any consultant by his first name but, after all, they were not on duty now!

'They both are, Findlay,' she replied, glancing quickly at his profile. 'They brought me up and have been like parents to me in every way. I could never repay them.'

His next words seemed to follow on naturally, with no hint of intrusion into her privacy. 'So—you lost your mother, then, Jenny?'

She hesitated for a second, and then replied, 'Yes, I'm afraid so, but please don't feel that you have to say anything. I don't remember her.' There's no way I'm going to wreck this evening with a recital of my dreary family saga, she thought.

'Ah, yes. I see.' He nodded as if he completely understood, which made her feel a little uncomfortable. Once again he seemed to be able to read her thoughts.

'I would guess that Grannie and Grampy feel well repaid by a lovely, caring granddaughter,' he said smilingly. 'Love is always a two-way blessing!'

'Thank you,' she murmured in some confusion. 'All I want right now is to see Grampy fit enough to come home again and Grannie smiling. But he's not doing very well so far, and Dennis—that's his son, my uncle—thinks he'll have to stay in the Hylton annexe permanently. He could be right.'

She sighed and shook her head doubtfully. The brief and unsuccessful home visit had disappointed both Grannie and herself, dashing their hopes of an early return to normality. She confided this episode to Findlay, and he looked thoughtful.

'Perhaps your Uncle Dennis could talk to him, man

to man on an equal footing. Let him know that when he's got this toilet problem under control he can go home, *but* that Mrs Curtis has to be considered, too, and can't be expected to give him the round-the-clock care that he's got used to. He might take it better, coming from his son.'

Jenny looked unconvinced. 'I'm not sure. They're not as close as some fathers and sons, and Dennis was really embarrassed when Grampy got so upset about having to go back to the annexe after spending Saturday afternoon at home. He's inclined to talk down to Grampy, or over his head as if he wasn't there.'

'Ah, too many people treat their elderly relatives like that,' said Findlay, shaking his head slowly. 'As you say, it's quite often due to embarrassment. Old people should be encouraged to accept responsibility for themselves, and given a chance to exercise their independence whenever it's possible. Perhaps you could have a word with your uncle, Jenny. Do you see much of him?'

'Not a great deal since he married and went to live down in Somerset,' she replied. 'He and his wife have two children, and they've invited Grannie and me to—'

She broke off in mid-sentence as they arrived at the gates of Stretbury Manor. 'Oh, we're here! Isn't it a lovely old place? I've never been inside it before.'

Lady Margaret greeted them at the front door, wearing a long skirt and a silk blouse with a shawl. Jenny felt conscious of her own exposed knees beneath the skimpy black skirt which had looked so smart in the shop.

'Come and meet my other guests,' said Lady Margaret as she led them into the lounge, where Jenny's heart sank a little at seeing Anne McGuire in an ankle-length, dark blue maternity gown, seated on a long settee with a glass of orange juice in her hand, and Conor hovering protectively nearby. The only other guest was a very old retired major who was introduced as a friend of Lady Margaret's father.

'Now, Conor, you must do the honours and pour a drink for our newcomers,' beamed the genial lady JP. 'I'm sure we've all got lots to ask them, and by the end of dinner we shall all know each other very much better!'

Jenny caught Findlay's eye momentarily, to be met with a half-smile. Privately she thought that they could be in for a heavy evening. They sat down on the settee together, Conor on Jenny's other side and Anne next to him. The major dozed peacefully in an armchair by the fire, and Lady Margaret stood leaning against the mantelpiece.

'Now, I know we all want to hear from Mr d'Arc about his locum consultancy,' she began in her magisterial tones. 'You needn't try to be modest, sir, because I've done my homework! You're a graduate of Edinburgh University, and trained in obstetrics at the Simpson Pavilion. You had a prestigious practice in Paris for several years, and you've practised in other European cities, notably Venice—from where you disappeared two years ago into the Brazilian jungle!

'But now you have resurfaced in our area just when we needed you. We're all interested to know why you've decided to leave your wonderful work in the Third World to come here!'

Findlay d'Arc, this is your life! thought Jenny, wondering how the consultant would respond to her ladyship's bulldozing tactics. Good old Lady Maggie had certainly got a nerve, but Jenny was dying to hear his answers.

Findlay sipped his dry sherry. 'You have indeed done your homework, Lady Hylton. The reason I came to Bristol was because there was a vacancy in the Department of Obstetrics and Gynaecology, following Mr Steynes's departure, and my application was successful.'

'And what were you doing in Brazil, Mr d'Arc?' asked Anne McGuire curiously.

'I was stationed at a small hospital that served a large area, Mrs McGuire,' he replied matter-of-factly. 'I practised both in the hospital and with the mobile clinic that went out to villages—a good life, and tremendous experience in all branches of medicine.'

'Were you under contract to the Brazilian government?' asked Conor.

'No, I was employed by the missionary society which ran the hospital. They needed an obstetrician to take care of their maternity patients, and I needed a complete change—and I got it! Everything from delivering babies to extracting teeth, not to mention malnutrition, dehydration and all the diseases that go with poverty. I'd recommend the life to anybody feeling jaded with Western values.'

'Is that a fact, Mr d'Arc? So what brought ye back to these decadent shores?' enquired Dr McGuire with a wink at his wife.

'I went down with a dose of viral hepatitis which everybody, including myself, thought was yellow fever—ugh!' Findlay shuddered ruefully at the memory. 'They pulled me through it, but it left me with a low red cell count that wouldn't respond to any treatment, and I was advised to get away from the tropics. So here I am, fit and ready to enjoy the next six months at Bristol. Mind you, I didn't anticipate the connection with Stretbury Memorial when I got the consultancy!'

'And are you pleased about that, Mr d'Arc?' asked Anne.

'I look upon it as an unexpected bonus, Mrs McGuire.'

'And do you plan to go back to Brazil when your six months are up?' asked Lady Margaret.

He smiled and shook his head. 'Which of us can foretell the future? It depends on many factors.'

'Well, I'm sure we all hope that you can be persuaded to stay and renew your contract, Mr d'Arc,' smiled her ladyship. 'And now let's turn to Sister Curtis, who has impressed us all after just one week at our hospital. What shall we call you, my dear—Jennifer?'

'Oh, Jenny, please.'

Here we go, she thought, my turn for the hot seat. Let's see if I can do as well as Findlay, and not give anything away!

'You told me at your interview that you had an interesting ward sister's post at the hospital where Mr d'Arc is now a consultant,' began Lady Margaret. 'I know you've come here to be near to your dear grandparents, and may I say how much we all hope that your grandfather is making good progress in the Hylton annexe?

'I believe you grew up in their home, Bailey's Cottage, which was once part of the Hylton estate—so, in effect, this is a homecoming for you, isn't it?'

While Jenny smiled and got ready to make a suitable reply Anne McGuire gave an exclamation.

'Curtis, that's *it*! I *knew* I ought to know you, Jenny,

because I'm a local girl as well, and did my training in
Bristol like you—only I'm a few years older so we
weren't there at the same time.'

Jenny looked up at her uncertainly, and only just remembered to smile.

'I—er—don't think I remember you, Mrs McGuire.'

'Anne—Anne Brittain as I was then.'

Jenny could only think of the former Miss Brittain's
reputation for single-minded efficiency, not to mention
bossiness, as Senior Nursing Administrator at Stretbury
Memorial so did not reply but went on smiling, quite
happy to give up the spotlight to her predecessor.

'I was at Stretbury Junior School with a Dennis Curtis
who lived at Bailey's Cottage,' went on Anne, narrowing
her eyes in an effort to delve into her memory. 'He was
a couple of years older than me. And wasn't there a
Cathy Curtis who lived there, an older sister of his? Yes,
she married a doctor and emigrated to Australia, didn't
she? My mother said that she—er—oh, dear me, er—'

Anne suddenly broke off and bit her lip. Her face
flushed crimson as she realised where her meandering
trail of reminiscence had led.

There was an extremely uncomfortable silence, during
which Conor poked his wife in the ribs and Lady Hylton
gasped in dismay. Jenny swallowed, then took a deep
breath and looked straight at Anne.

'You're correct so far, Mrs McGuire. Cathy Curtis
married a doctor from New South Wales and went off
with him, leaving the baby behind. Are there any further
details you'd like me to fill in, or will somebody else
volunteer to have their private matters dissected in public?'

Anne McGuire wilted visibly under the sarcasm that

Jenny could not keep out of her voice, and their hostess hastened to smooth things over.

'My dear Jenny, you mustn't think—Anne didn't intend, I'm sure— We're all waiting to hear your impressions of Stretbury Memorial. I hear that you're tremendously popular on the men's ward, and Mr Gould says he wishes he could have his operation under your care. Do you think there's any chance of Mr Jamieson agreeing to that?'

Jenny was about to say that she had no idea but, to her utter dismay, she found that her mouth had gone dry and no sound came out.

I must be gaping like a dying codfish, she thought in panic, and lowered her eyes to her lap where she saw that her hands were shaking as she held her half-full wineglass. This is ridiculous, she told herself. For heaven's sake, give her an answer, *any* answer, you idiot…

But no answer was forthcoming, and her panic increased as a wave of dizziness swept over her.

And then her glass was deftly removed from her hand and placed on a low table beside the settee. The next thing she felt was Findlay d'Arc's arm firmly around her shoulders, and she heard his voice—courteous, pleasant and absolutely in command.

'Miss Curtis has been under a great deal of pressure in her new post, Lady Hylton, and should surely now be allowed to relax and enjoy this evening in the company of colleagues and friends. I am sure that you all understand.'

There was a moment of complete, open-mouthed silence, broken by the major who woke with a start and gave a loud snort. Conor McGuire had to put his hand to his mouth to hide a grin, and Lady Hylton was all apologies.

'Er—oh, yes, of course, how unforgivable of me. Let me see, it's nearly eight o'clock so shall we go into the dining-room now?' she suggested.

Findlay rose at once. 'I'm sure we're all looking forward to sampling your hospitality, Lady Hylton,' he said with friendly politeness, as if he had not just given her a mild rebuke. He offered her his arm, while Conor winked at Jenny and offered her his. That left Anne McGuire to guide the major's faltering steps as they followed the others.

The meal was as lavish as it was delicious, and over the soup, salmon mousse, roast pork and a variety of vegetables the talk was fairly general. Jenny felt more than a little out of her depth with such matters as the day-to-day running of a small NHS trust hospital and the seasonal demands of a large rural general practice.

Once again she found that her appetite had deserted her, and took only small helpings which she ate slowly.

When the men began to discuss cars Findlay mentioned his newly purchased saloon and its low fuel consumption. Jenny remarked that her uncle's car was an older model of the same make.

'He says he can make the journey up from Dewsfold in under two hours, going via Taunton and the M5,' she said. 'He's coming to fetch my grandmother and me to his daughter's birthday party the weekend after next.'

'Good heavens, what a coincidence!' exclaimed Findlay. 'I'm driving down to Lyme Regis that weekend to see my parents. I stayed with them when I first arrived in England, and it's time I visited them again. Yes, the A358 goes through Axminster, which is near Dewsfold, isn't it? I could give you and Mrs Curtis a lift and save your brother the journey.'

Jenny could hardly believe her ears. 'But Mr d'Arc—er—Findlay, we couldn't possibly impose on you, all that way!'

'No problem, I'd be glad of your company,' he assured her, apparently unaware of the glances that were being exchanged between Lady Margaret and the McGuires. 'When would you prefer to travel—Friday evening or Saturday morning?'

'I—I think Friday—whatever suits you,' stammered Jenny.

'Friday will be fine. Only—you had better not make any arrangements to go out to dinner that evening.'

His blue eyes gleamed as Jenny blushed at this reference to Steve Forrest, while Lady Margaret commented on the happy chance that enabled Mr d'Arc to provide transport for Jenny and her grandmother just when they needed it.

After dinner coffee was served in the lounge, and Jenny slipped away upstairs to the bathroom where she grimaced at her reflection in the mirror and ran a comb through her unruly mop. A knock at the door announced Anne McGuire, who had followed her upstairs. She was clearly very agitated.

'Jenny, I can't tell you how sorry I am, putting my foot in it like that. Honestly, I had no idea—I'm an idiot,' she apologised.

Jenny did not contradict her, and Anne floundered on.

'I do hope that you'll forgive me, Jenny. I'd very much like us to be friends.'

Jenny faced her squarely. 'Look, when you're not sure of your facts the best course is to say nothing, especially

in front of strangers. You can hardly blame me for an-
swering back.'

'Oh, *please* don't be angry. I can see you're hurt—'

'Never mind about hurt—you've shown me up as a
fool in front of Mr d'Arc,' muttered Jenny, and Anne
looked bewildered. 'All right, then, let's say no more
about it, OK?'

'That's very good of you,' said Anne in an unusually
subdued tone for her, and Jenny noticed the rapid rise
and fall of the low-cut maternity dress. Careful, this is
an elderly primigravida whose blood pressure mustn't go
up, whether I like her or not, she reminded herself. Her
features softened into a friendly grin.

'All right, Anne, don't worry. Just take care of yourself and young McGuire in there. Come on, let's get
back to the company. The major'll be missing me!'

On the return drive Jenny felt that an explanation was
due to Findlay, and she plunged straight into it.

'Thank you for coming to my rescue back there,
Findlay, I know that Anne McGuire didn't deliberately
intend to show me up like that, but I could have throttled
her just the same. You must have thought—'

'There is no need to say any more,' he cut in quickly.
'I was sorry for you *and* Mrs McGuire! She will be more
careful in future, I'm sure.'

'No, I'd like to set the record straight,' insisted Jenny.
'You asked me if I had lost my mother, and I said I had.
That was true, though not in the way it sounded. She
was a student nurse of twenty when I came along and I
was going to be adopted, but when she—well, when
Grannie and Grampy saw me they said they'd look after
me while she finished her training.'

He looked straight ahead as he replied. 'All right, then, Jenny. Tell me all about it.'

She drew in a sharp breath. His quietly spoken words had the effect of unleashing a torrent of painful emotions that Jenny had not acknowledged for years, still less expressed. She began to pour out her feelings as never before.

'Trouble was, it didn't last very long, not as far as Cathy Curtis was concerned, you see. My father was supposed to have been a medical student, though he might just as well have been the mortuary attendant, for all I know.

'At any rate, he melted away like morning dew when she told him her not-so-good news. When she went back to finish training, guess what? She met this gorgeous hunk, an anaesthetist from New South Wales, and it was love at first sight. He wanted to whisk her back with him to the Land of Oz, only he didn't fancy having a little howling bundle as part of the deal so she went and I stayed. That's about it, really.'

Findlay nodded slowly, still keeping his eyes on the road. 'I see. So she lives in Australia now.'

'Yes, they got married and have three kids of their own, maybe four. I can't remember.' Jenny's tone was brittle.

'So you don't keep in touch?'

She shrugged. 'Christmas and birthday cards.'

'And you've never seen her again?'

There was a pause before she answered. 'Yes. They came over about twelve years ago on a visit. It was a bit of a disaster, really. I was fourteen—too old to be her little girl, and too young to cope with it, I suppose. I just stuck to Grannie and hardly opened my mouth.

'She—my mother—had brought presents for me, really nice things, but I wouldn't unwrap them or say thank you or anything. Poor Grannie, it must have been a nightmare for her, me behaving like that. It wasn't much fun all round.'

She cleared her throat. 'And, actually, it must have been pretty awful for her, too—Cathy, my mother.'

I mustn't get tearful whatever happens, she told herself, or my mascara will run. She stole a peep at Findlay's profile as he drove. His expression was thoughtful, and he said nothing for about a minute. Then he spoke softly.

'I'm so pleased to hear that last thing you said, Jenny, about your mother's difficulties. Your disappointing response to her was understandable, of course, and one could even say that she deserved it after her desertion of you. But she has to carry the lifelong burden of what happened while you can forgive her, and that sets you free, doesn't it? Do you see what I mean?'

'Er—yes, I suppose I do,' she muttered.

But I haven't forgiven her, she thought silently, and you know that I haven't, you mind-reading wizard. She closed her eyes as she faced this fact, and marvelled at the way she had told this man so much. It was a subject she had never mentioned to Steve.

'Oh, just listen to me, coming out with all this old stuff!' she said with an attempt at a laugh. 'I'm sorry, Findlay, I really am!'

'*I'm* not,' he said with a quick sideways glance. 'I'm very glad that you've felt able to tell me. To be honest, I thought it might be something like that.'

'I don't think I've ever told anybody the full story before,' she admitted. 'I've never spoken to Grannie and

Grampy about how I feel—I mean, about *her*. After all, she is their daughter, and they lost her too.'

'Ah, but they've had you to take her place, Jenny.'

'And I've had them,' she answered, as if following his train of thought.

She lay back in the passenger seat, closing her eyes and letting the tensions of the evening drain from her body, leaving her tired but relaxed. There was no need to put on any kind of an act with this man. Was it only a week since they had met? And tomorrow they would be working together again in the little theatre on the Tuesday gynae list.

She suddenly wondered how Steve Forrest had spent the evening, and gave a little chuckle at the memory of the double date. Poor Steve! He had taken it very well, and she would have to make it up to him in some way soon...

On their arrival back at Bailey's Cottage Findlay got out of the car and came with her to the front door. The sky was clear, and a three-quarter moon hung above the summit of Stretbury Hill. There was a sweet, earthy fragrance in the air, and Findlay drew in a deep breath, exhaling it slowly.

'This was what I missed in the tropics, Jenny, the English countryside's awakening in spring. To me it's the most beautiful time of the year—when the earth seems to be holding her breath, ready to burst forth into new life!'

He put a hand on her shoulder as he pointed towards Stretbury Hill. 'See those big old trees up there with their bare branches against the sky? Any day now those millions of tiny leaf-buds will break open and cover the branches with a green mist—the new foliage of another summer.'

He inhaled deeply again, and she saw his lean features soften. In the semi-darkness the lines etched by experience and some past sorrow were no longer visible, and he seemed much younger. His eyes, darkened by night, had lost their sombre look and shone with appreciation of the present moment.

He looks simply devastating, Jenny realised in a sudden heart-stopping moment of revelation. I've actually been out with this man tonight, and what a bore I've been—what a *drip*, picking at my food and droning on about my dreary life history!

She could have kicked herself, yet at the same time she was overwhelmingly grateful for the understanding he had shown, not least his intervention during the hideous embarrassment of the pre-dinner conversation.

'Thank you for everything, Findlay,' she said simply. 'I didn't think I'd enjoy it but, thanks to you, it was, er—what's the word?'

'Interesting?' he suggested, and she gave a peal of laughter.

'That's as good as any I can think of!'

She held out her hands, and he turned to look at her. Something in the depths of his eyes, softly gleaming in the moonlight, arrested her so completely that she neither spoke nor moved, but remained facing him, her hands still outstretched and her eyes questioning, waiting for him to speak.

'You were made for happiness, Jenny, not bitterness. You have a gift for laughter, for enjoying life, and you must never lose it. It's much too precious.'

She stood before him for an endless minute, and then,

without any deliberation on her part, her arms rose to rest upon his shoulders. Slowly they moved forward, curving around his neck. She stood on tiptoe and he leaned a little towards her so that at last their heads rested side by side, their ears touching. She felt his crisp, shaggy hair against her short crop, and was aware of the warmth of his body through the well-tailored suit.

Surely he must feel her pounding heart as his arms enfolded her waist, holding her in a light embrace—not tightly but close enough to envelop her in an aura of warmth and security. She breathed in the lingering carnation tang of his soap on the skin that just touched her cheek...

For a few moments he stood quite still, holding her as if acknowledging all that she had tried to say, and then he gently withdrew his arms and straightened. Her arms fell back, and once again they were separate and apart.

'Ah, Jenny,' he said softly. 'I *have* enjoyed this evening—well, most of it!'

He smiled and patted her shoulder. 'And now we must say goodnight, little Jenny. Sleep well.'

'Good night, Findlay,' she breathed as he walked away. At the gate he turned and gave a wave, before disappearing behind the tall hedge. She heard him unlocking the car.

Jenny went indoors and walked upstairs in a dream. What had happened this evening? They hadn't kissed or whispered anything romantic. Their brief contact had been merely a hug, not much more than the sort she gave Grampy. Nothing more than that.

And yet her heart was in a turmoil such as no words could describe. She had told him so much about herself, though she still knew absolutely nothing about his own personal history.

From the window of her room she saw the red rear lights of his car disappearing round the corner of the green.

'Findlay,' she whispered. 'Oh, Findlay d'Arc, what must you think of me? Throwing myself at you like that—I must be going balmy!'

And for a long while she gazed wonderingly at the night sky and the silent rural scene bathed in moonlight.

CHAPTER FOUR

ON TUESDAY morning Jenny arrived on duty half an hour early to give herself time to take the night report and do a round of her patients in the men's ward, before handing them over to Staff Nurse Barnett and going to prepare the theatre for the gynae op list which began at nine.

'Morning, Sister Curtis! I hear that you were dining at Stretbury Manor last night,' remarked Doreen Nixon as soon as she entered the theatre. 'How was Lady Hylton's hospitality?'

'News soon gets around in this place, Doreen. Good job I managed to hold out against the major's passionate advances, or you'd all be talking about my downfall this morning,' grinned Jenny.

Doreen laughed. 'A major, eh? Does Dr Forrest know he's got a rival?'

Jenny did not reply, but felt a secret tremor run down her spine, and knew that it was not because Steve Forrest was soon due to arrive. The thought of facing Findlay d'Arc after the odd little scene last night had set her heart fluttering in case there should be any embarrassment.

'Two hysterectomies, two laparoscopic sterilisations and two D and Cs—that should keep us well occupied,' Doreen went on. 'It's a funny thing, Sister, this time last week I just couldn't imagine anybody but Mr Steynes doing these Tuesday lists, but now I'm really looking forward to seeing Mr d'Arc again!'

'Yes, I'll say!' added Jill as she joined them. 'He's really rather gorgeous, isn't he? And such perfect manners!'

'Ah, the fickle heart of woman,' Jenny murmured.

'Is he married, d'you know, Sister?' asked Jill.

'Presumably not, if he's just come back from overseas service in the Third World and lives alone in Bristol,' replied Jenny lightly, not wanting to appear interested in Findlay's personal life, though privately she shared Jill's curiosity.

'But surely there *must* have been some women in his life,' insisted the romantic Jill. 'I have this feeling that there was someone very special at one time in his past—don't you think so, Sister?'

Jenny frowned in concentration on her instrument trolley, and the nurses took the hint, bustling around at their own tasks—which included placing the newly acquired patient slide ready beside the operating table. Dr McGuire could be heard whistling in the adjoining anaesthetic room, and Jill hurried to assist him as two pairs of footsteps were heard approaching the theatre.

'Good morning, Sister Curtis—Nurse Nixon,' said Findlay cordially as he entered dressed in theatre blues and with a surgical cap and mask on. 'We have a new obstetric house surgeon this morning, Dr Diana Rowland, who has come to assist me.'

Dr Rowland was a shy-looking girl who smiled at them above her mask. Findlay explained that Dr Forrest had been up for much of the night in the delivery unit.

'As Dr Rowland is new on the team I thought I'd bring her to see an example of a small hospital with a high standard of care,' he went on in his politely formal manner. 'Right, Sister Curtis, if Dr McGuire is ready with our first patient Dr Rowland and I will scrub up.'

Jenny nodded. 'Very well, sir.' There was clearly no place for secret flutterings in such a coolly efficient atmosphere.

In spite of her inexperience the new house surgeon proved to be quick to learn under Findlay's unobtrusive instruction, and Jenny had to be especially alert to their requirements and ready to act as assistant surgeon when necessary.

When the list was completed and the last patient wheeled out of the little theatre, Jenny pulled off her cap, gloves and mask and gave a brief nod of acknowledgement to the two doctors.

'Wait, Sister Curtis, I have a note for you,' Findlay called to her. 'It's in my jacket pocket—excuse me a minute.'

He disappeared into the small office used by male theatre staff for changing, and returned with an envelope.

'It's from Dr Forrest—he asked me to give it to you,' he said with a half-smile. 'It's not often that I get asked to play Cupid!'

Jenny gasped and blushed to the roots of her hair, still wild and uncombed after being pushed under a theatre cap. What was Steve thinking of? As if last night's scene had not been bad enough!

'Sorry, Mr d'Arc,' she muttered. 'He shouldn't have bothered you with it.'

Doreen and Jill exchanged significant looks as they cleared and cleaned the theatre. As Jenny turned to leave Findlay asked her if she was going to the dining-room for lunch.

'Er—no, not straight away, sir,' she answered, realising that once again she had lost her appetite.

'Were you thinking of visiting the Hylton annexe, Sister? If so, I'd like to come with you—that is, if you don't mind.'

'What? Why, no—I mean, yes, of course, Mr d'Arc,' she replied, her face lighting up. 'I won't take two ticks to change into uniform—'

'I'll show Dr Rowland the way to the dining-room, and then join you in the annexe, Sister.'

Doreen and Jill exchanged another look.

Grampy seemed no happier. He had been sitting out on the covered verandah of the annexe, overlooking the spacious grounds which were maintained by a full-time gardener who had a series of young and inexperienced assistants supplied by a youth training scheme.

'I've been watching that fool of a boy messing about all the morning in the greenhouse over there,' Will Curtis grumbled. 'He's got no idea! Why they let these daft youngsters loose on jobs they know nothing about, heaven only knows. Nothing but a waste o' time and people's money.'

'Now, Grampy, forget about the boy and meet Mr d'Arc,' said Jenny soothingly, kissing his cheek. 'He comes over from Bristol to do operations—he's a surgeon.'

'Oh, ah? I reckon I've had enough o' doctors to see me out,' muttered Grampy, without looking up, and Jenny gave Findlay an apologetic shrug. To her surprise, he laughed out loud.

'Well said, Mr Curtis! Half the time they don't know what they're talking about, do they? It's like that boy in the greenhouse, with no idea of what he should be doing! And, what's more, nobody shows him, do they? Ridiculous system, isn't it?'

Jenny stared up at him in amazement. Was he serious, or was he—? Heaven forbid, he surely wasn't making fun of poor old miserable Grampy, was he?

'I'll tell you what, Mr Curtis,' Findlay went on in a confiding tone. 'That young lad needs somebody with a bit of know-how and some time to spare to steer him in the right direction, if you see what I mean. What do you think, Jenny?'

'Yes, I suppose he does, really—if somebody could be found who was willing to— Oh, *Findlay!*' she cried as light dawned on her, and she spun round to face him. 'Are you thinking what I'm—?'

'Shh!' He put his finger to his lips. 'The question is, what does Mr Curtis think?'

He sat down beside the old man who at last gave him a grudging nod. Jenny sat on Grampy's other side and took his hand.

'Listen, Grampy, dear, how would *you* like to lend a hand in that greenhouse? You're a dab hand at seed propagation, and you've got so much knowledge to share. Why, you could grow tomatoes in there for the patients in the annexe! I'll get you anything you need from home—'

'Too early to plant out tomatoes yet—leave 'em till mid-May, else the frost'll have 'em,' growled Grampy.

'Yes, Will, that's just what I say—these idiots *will* go and plant out too soon,' agreed Findlay gloomily. 'Just because they see a ray of spring sunshine they forget about the freezing nights still to come, and bang goes the lot.' He shook his head sadly from side to side in a way that nearly convulsed Jenny, who muttered out of the corner of her mouth to him.

'All right, all right, don't overdo it!' Raising her voice, she spoke encouragingly to Grampy.

'Look, I'm going to ask Sister Mason if you can be spared for an hour each day to be—er—greenhouse gardener—'

'And instructor,' put in Findlay.

'Yes, that's right, instructor—and see what improvements you can make. How do you like the idea?'

The old man looked doubtful, but a gleam appeared in his eye.

'I'd need my own tools from home. And there's another thing, Doctor,' he added to Findlay in a lowered tone, not meant for female ears.

'What's that, Will?'

'I'd have to take one o' them screw-top jars with me just in case I had to go in a hurry, if you follow me, Doctor.'

'I'm sure that could be arranged, Will.'

And it was arranged by Jenny that same afternoon. Will Curtis put on his outdoor shoes, ancient jacket and peaked cap and was escorted by an unconvinced Sister Mason to the greenhouse, where he was introduced to Andrew, the latest recruit from the YTS—a rather withdrawn boy whose life had been shattered by his parents' break-up.

It was an unpromising start but, looking back later, Jenny always insisted that it was the day her grandfather turned the corner and began his rehabilitation.

'Honestly, Findlay, I nearly exploded when you talked about gardening,' she chuckled as they walked back to the main building. 'And that's the first time he's ever admitted to having a bladder problem.'

'It just goes to show that we must never give up hope, Sister,' Findlay said gently. 'Give Will a little more time, and don't assume that deterioration is inevitable. Improvement can and does occur in seemingly hopeless cases, you know. Time and time again the behaviour of the elderly confused has been known to improve with the right kind of management.'

Jenny was heartened by these encouraging words, and warmed by Findlay's undoubted interest in the problem that affected the whole Curtis family.

'I can't wait to tell Dr Sellars about this!' she said happily.

'Be tactful,' he cautioned, 'or he'll be telling me to stick to gynaecology!'

With a nod he turned on his heel and made for the car park, leaving Jenny to reflect once again on his insight.

It was not until visiting time on the men's ward that Jenny sat down in the office and opened Steve's letter, shaking her head at the way he had used Findlay as a postman. What a cheek!

'Darling Jenny,' the note began. 'Terribly disappointed over not seeing you today. I'd have come over as usual, but I suspect that our friend Findlay wanted to show off his skill to the new girl on the team.'

He went on to suggest a visit to the cinema at Wotton-under-Edge, where an award-winning film was being shown that week.

'Just give me a buzz on my mobile phone, and we'll

fix a date,' he wrote. 'Missing you, darling—all my love, Steve.'

It had been quickly scribbled on hospital notepaper, and Jenny squirmed at the thought of a consultant surgeon being used to carry messages between a houseman and his girlfriend. Steve assumed too much, she decided, and because there were a lot of problems on the men's ward that day she forgot to call him back.

When he telephoned her at Bailey's Cottage that night she accepted his suggestion about seeing the film of Jane Austen's *Sense and Sensibility*, and told him of Grampy's new interest as hospital greenhouse assistant. He agreed that it was a splendid idea and congratulated her.

'Oh, it was Mr d'Arc's suggestion! It's all thanks to him,' she emphasised.

'D'Arc? How did *he* get involved? Straying a bit from his speciality, isn't he?'

'Mr d'Arc's interested in *everybody*, and he sees patients as people first and foremost,' said Jenny firmly. 'That includes every aspect of their lives, not just their current state of health, and he—'

'Sure, the holistic approach. I'm quite into holistic medicine myself,' Steve hastened to tell her. 'Only how did our friend Findlay know about your grandfather's problems?'

'Because I *told* him, of course, Steve, though everybody at Stretbury Memorial seems to know that Grampy's in the annexe and that's why I changed my job. It's no secret!'

'Of course, darling Jenny, and I'm just thrilled for the old boy, naturally. You know how much I care about everything that concerns you.'

But not enough to visit Grampy yourself and give some practical help and advice, she reflected silently.

Grannie passed by on her way upstairs to bed.

'I'd better go now, Steve,' said Jenny. 'I'll see you on Thursday at seven, then.'

'I can hardly wait. Goodnight, darling. Sleep well.'

On Thursday afternoon the staff-midwife who usually helped at the antenatal clinic had to stay on the maternity ward with a patient in labour so Sister Garrett asked Jenny to take her place while an auxiliary nurse chaperoned Mr d'Arc.

Jenny received the mothers as they arrived, weighed them, took their blood pressure and tested urine samples. She also took blood samples from new bookings and as requested by Findlay and Sister Garrett. The latter was clearly impressed by Jenny's unhurried efficiency, and told her so at the end of the clinic.

'You've been a godsend, Sister Curtis. I really had no idea when I asked you to chaperon Mr d'Arc last week—'

'Think nothing of it, Sister,' replied naughty Jenny. 'Last Thursday I spent my time changing paper sheets and pulling up knickers, and this week I'm promoted to junior lab assistant. Who knows where my meteoric career will end up? Perhaps I'll be allowed to—' She broke off quickly as the consultant approached. 'Oh, good afternoon, Mr d'Arc.'

'Ah, there you are, Sister Curtis. I've missed you, but I assume that you've had more important work to do today.'

His twinkling eyes belied his matter-of-fact manner,

and Jenny sheepishly mumbled that she had to return to her ward.

'Wait a moment, Sister,' he called, striding after her. 'How are the seedlings coming on under the new management?'

'I haven't had a chance to look in today,' she replied a little breathlessly. 'Yesterday I brought in his trowels and fork and things—'

'And is he using them, Jenny? Shall we go and see?'

Jenny needed no persuading, and as they approached the annexe by the garden path he suddenly laid a restraining hand on her arm, which made her catch her breath.

'Look over there, Jenny—in the greenhouse—see?'

She followed the direction of his pointing finger, and gave a little gasp.

Andrew had his back to them, and his attention was centred on the seed-trays set out before him. Beside him on a high stool sat Grampy in his shirt-sleeves, leaning forward to demonstrate some point to the boy. Andrew turned and said something to the old man, which must have amused them both because Grampy raised a fist in mock fury and Andrew clapped him on the shoulder. Then they both reapplied their attention to the work in hand.

'Master and pupil, eh?' grinned Findlay, drawing Jenny aside towards a large rhododendron bush covered with tiny buds that would burst into bloom in a few weeks' time. 'Careful, don't let them see us.'

'Oh, Findlay—' Jenny was momentarily overcome, and her voice broke on a little sob. 'This idea of yours is doing the trick! Grannie will be so happy— Oh, I'm sorry, but this has just made my day…'

And as her emotion spilled over Findlay drew her close, and in the concealment of the bush she impulsively threw her arms around his neck. He felt her tears warm against his cheek, a healing stream that went straight to the source of a long-hidden sorrow. His arms tightened around her.

'All right, Jenny, all right,' he murmured against her hair. A tremor in his voice made her raise her head to look into his face and she saw, to her dismay, that his own deep blue eyes were glittering with unshed tears.

'Findlay! Oh, Mr d'Arc, what is it?' she asked anxiously, her own concerns immediately forgotten. 'Is there something wrong, or have I—?'

He smiled and shook his head as he continued to hold her against him so that she was conscious of his heartbeat.

'It's all right, little Jenny, it's nothing you've said or done. You've just made me think of another time, that's all. Someone I loved deeply, and lost—it's all right, don't worry.'

As he cleared his throat and drew a long breath Jenny was overwhelmed by an aching tenderness towards this man, who was holding her in his arms and remembering this *someone* that she knew nothing about. She longed with all her heart to comfort him, and with a woman's sure instinct she pressed her soft lips against his cheek in a child-like kiss.

'Dear little Jenny,' he breathed, and she felt his own lips touch her wet cheek. The sensation was electrifying.

'Findlay—oh, Findlay d'Arc—'

It was only the slightest turn of her head that brought his mouth close to hers, and then their lips were touching. Jenny closed her eyes and gave herself up to a kiss that seemed to draw her into the very heart of the man. She sensed a tremendous yearning in it that could never have been put into words, as if a long-pent-up river had begun to find release. For an endless moment time stood still, but at length it passed and he slowly released her, drawing a long, shuddering breath.

'Oh, my God, Jenny,' he whispered, so softly that she hardly heard. 'Dear Jenny, forgive me.'

Her heart cried out that there was nothing to forgive, but no words came and she lowered her eyes for fear of giving away too much of what she felt.

'You're a lovely girl, Jenny,' he went on in a lighter tone, 'and Dr Forrest is a very lucky man. Thank you for being so sweet, but I cannot burden you with…' He hesitated for a moment, then smiled and patted her shoulder. 'And I'm so pleased about Grampy's new job!'

And that was all. He left her side and walked rapidly towards the car park, while she returned to the men's ward and resumed her duties there as if nothing had happened, though her thoughts were in a whirl of confusion and uncertainty.

She could not work up much enthusiasm for the evening with Steve, a prospect which would have filled her with eager anticipation three months ago—or even six weeks. Yet now that the attractive young doctor seemed to have become so interested in her she no longer seemed to know her own mind or what she wanted.

Getting ready to go to the cinema, she told herself not to be daft. The really big news was that Grampy was starting to improve at last—after she had practically given up hope. And what could be more important than that?

* * *

Steve reached out and took her hand as they sat in the cinema, watching the classic romance in which the heroine couldn't be sure of the hero's true feelings. Jenny sympathised with her, but became a little impatient as the story progressed.

'What did you think of it, darling?' asked Steve later, when they were sitting in his car.

'Oh, I loved it, Steve—only I think if I'd been her I'd have shaken him till his teeth rattled and told him to come to the point!'

She immediately regretted the words when he entwined his fingers with hers and asked with a meaningful look if she felt the same way about him.

'Because I could come to the point at any time you like, darling,' he murmured, his lips against her right ear. 'Where would you like to go now? There's a place I know in Clifton that does a nice little late supper—'

'Oh, no, Steve, I must go home, honestly,' she said quickly. 'I'm up at six-thirty, remember! Look, why don't you come back to Bailey's Cottage and let me do poached eggs on toast?'

'That's sweet of you, Jenny, but your grandmother will be there, won't she?'

Precisely, thought Jenny, who had definitely decided that she was not ready for any serious commitments just yet.

April gave way to May and the days sped by, leaving Jenny little time to ponder over romantic involvements. Findlay was pleasantly cordial, but no reference was made to the episode in the shadow of the rhododendron bush, and all that aching, tender passion in a kiss meant for Someone Else. Much as she longed to know about the past love which still overshadowed his life, it was clear that he was not able or willing to share it. Meanwhile, she secretly counted the days to the weekend at Dewsfold, and the journey in Findlay's car.

Steve continued to pursue her, and their colleagues clearly assumed that their relationship was serious. Any lack of response on her part only seemed to increase his interest, and it vaguely annoyed her that Findlay believed her to be as good as engaged to the young houseman. Once or twice she caught him looking at them across the operating table on Tuesday mornings, at which times he seldom addressed Steve directly, or gave him only the briefest of replies.

Jenny was quite relieved on the odd occasions when Diana Rowland assisted Findlay instead of Steve, and the theatre staff could not help noticing how much more cheerful and forthcoming the consultant was in her presence. Everybody liked her, and when she confided to Jenny and the nurses over coffee that she hoped to work in the Third World after qualifying Doreen and Jill exchanged looks and nudges. A nice, serious-minded girl like that would be an ideal companion for Mr You-know-who, they implied, and Findlay certainly seemed relaxed in her company.

When Diana asked Jenny if she was going to the midsummer party to be held in the medical quarters at the Bristol hospital, Jenny had to reply that she had been invited to go with Steve. There had seemed to be no good reason why she should not accept, particularly as it would be a good chance to see many of her old friends again, and catch up on Bristol news and gossip.

Even so, she was aware of a certain awkwardness in the theatre and Diana gave Findlay a look which Jenny could not interpret, nor could she understand why she found it so unsettling.

If Diana was the woman who could release Findlay d'Arc from the sorrow of the past, whatever it was, surely that was good and something to be glad about. Or so Jenny told herself, without much conviction.

Dr Sellars nodded approvingly when Jenny told him about her grandfather's new interest and the difference it had made to his mental state.

'Of course, the antidepressants are really beginning to take effect now. I'm feeling much more hopeful, Jenny.'

'I'm glad to hear that, Doctor,' she said, remembering his former pessimism.

'By the way, Mr Jamieson is asking if he can operate on Mr Gould here next week,' he went on. 'Apparently, they've had to cancel several ops through shortage of beds, and Gould himself is in favour. How do you feel about it?'

'Fine, Dr Sellars,' she replied. 'I'll be happy to look after Mr Gould all the way through.'

'Good, I'll let Jamieson know. Any other problems?'

'Er—no, Dr Sellars.'

He noticed the slight hesitation. 'Are you sure, Jenny? Is there anything you want to tell me?' he asked kindly.

'No, honestly, Doctor. Nothing.'

But when he had left the men's ward she sat down in the office and put a hand over the nagging pain in her tummy. By now Jenny was fairly certain that her intermittent discomfort and loss of appetite was due to an ongoing inflammatory condition of her appendix, a 'grumbling' that had bothered her on and off for several months.

Well, you'll just have to go on grumbling, she told it crossly. There was no way that she was going off sick during a staff crisis, with so many problems to be tackled. When the new senior nursing administrator arrived in September there would be time enough to worry about herself…

Findlay had arranged to call for Mrs Curtis and Jenny at six o'clock on the Friday evening, and drive them down to Dewsfold. Grannie had been undecided whether she should leave Grampy unvisited for a whole weekend, and only when he actually told her to attend Amanda's party did she finally agree to go.

'I've packed your best dress and jacket, Grannie, with your shoes, gloves, nightie, slippers and the presents for Amanda and William,' said Jenny, kneeling beside the case on the bedroom floor. 'Have you got your pills in your handbag? Heavens, there's the doorbell—he's here already, and I look a sight!'

She hastily threw a few clothes and toilet requisites into her own suitcase as she heard Grannie offering Findlay a cup of tea.

'There's some sponge cake to eat up, if you'd like it, Dr Findlay,' said the old lady, and Jenny winced. Just as well I've never set out to impress him, she thought, carrying her case downstairs and feeling unaccountably shy as she confronted the tall figure in the hallway.

'I hope we're not taking up all your space, Mr d'Arc,' she apologised.

'No problem. I've only packed a few casual things for loafing around,' he replied, and then stared disconcertingly at her, lifting his heavy eyebrows as if in surprise.

Do I look such a scruff? she wondered, little realising

that he was struck by the youthful, almost childlike picture she presented in a denim boiler suit with bib and braces, worn over a light cotton shirt. She looked about sixteen.

My God, how utterly sweet she is, Findlay was thinking. No wonder Forrest is enchanted by her! I only hope the man's half worthy of such a girl, and can make her as happy as she deserves.

'Right, then,' he said cheerfully, collecting his thoughts. 'Shall we put Mrs Curtis in the passenger seat beside me, and Jenny at the back with your handbags and hats?'

Jenny leaned back in her seat, prepared to enjoy the drive and the views of the Gloucestershire and Somerset countryside in the mellow evening light—not to mention the back of Findlay's head and his reflection in the driving-mirror as he listened to Grannie's chatty confidences.

'I should have had more sense with my Will, Dr Findlay,' she sighed. 'He's worked out of doors all his life, you see, but he's never lifted a finger in the house, and he didn't have enough to do, especially in the winter. I waited on him hand and foot, did everything for him, but he just got more bored and bad-tempered—I made a rod for my own back, and in the end I just couldn't cope any longer. He wasn't like my Will at all.'

Jenny sighed as Grannie opened her heart to this man, just as she herself had done, and wished that the old lady had been as willing to confide in her about Grampy's deterioration. Findlay was nodding as the sad story unfolded.

'And you felt that you had to cover up for your husband, didn't you, Mrs Curtis?' he commented gently, as much for Jenny's ears as her grandmother's.

'Yes, Doctor, and it was silly of me, I know that now. I should have asked for help before things got so bad.'

'Don't blame yourself, my dear. You meant it for the best, and you won't make the same mistake again,' Findlay said with a smile.

'I certainly won't when I get him home again, Dr Findlay,' Grannie declared. 'He's ever so much better now that he's got this poor boy, Andrew, to look after. You should hear what Will tells me about the life that lad's had since his mother left home. Oh, Dr Findlay, you don't know what it means to me to have my husband back again, almost like he used to be!'

Findlay chuckled softly, and Jenny gazed at his mirrored reflection with a dreamy smile—until the image winked at her, and she realised that he could see *her* reflection!

Good heavens! He must think I'm a nutcase, she thought, hastily straightening her features into what she hoped was an intelligent expression.

It was almost eight when they drew up outside the semi-detached house on a small estate. Dennis came out to take their cases, followed by Sheila, another young woman, Amanda and her eight-year-old brother William, and an excited little boy and girl. Sheila had a rather harassed air.

'Hello, hello, so glad you could come! This is my sister, Carol, and her pair of imps, Vicki and Simon— *shh*, everybody!'

Findlay took Mrs Curtis's arm to help her indoors, where the atmosphere was chaotic. Sheila handed round tea and biscuits while Vicki and Simon charged from room to room, screaming happily.

'We'll be having supper after this lot have gone to bed,' whispered Sheila, but was overheard.

The two imps roared in unison, 'Fish 'n' chips, fish 'n' chips from the shop!'

Jenny asked if there was anything she could do to help.

'Tomorrow's the problem,' explained Sheila apologetically. 'Dennis has got to work, and Carol and I have to do the rest of the shopping for the birthday lunch on Sunday—I'm doing a buffet, and there'll be lots of us. We need tons more food, and there's the cake to pick up. Amanda can come with us, but if you could stay here and mind William and these two it would be marvellous.'

'Of course,' replied Jenny promptly. 'We'll have some fun, won't we, William? You must help me with Vicki and—er—'

'I'm Sime!' yelled the four-year-old. 'Who are you?'

'I'm Jenny Poppins, and I've got a magic umbrella so you'd better watch out,' replied Jenny darkly.

In the ensuing shouts of 'Show us! Show us!' Findlay got up, thanked Sheila for the tea and said he had better be going. Jenny saw him to the door, her heart sinking.

'Thank you so much, Findlay,' she said gratefully, thinking how relieved he must be to escape.

'It's going to be a bit much for Grannie, don't you think?' he said thoughtfully as they stood at the door. 'Those three musketeers had better be taken out for a picnic tomorrow.'

They were immediately surrounded by William, Vicki and Simon.

'We're going for a picnic, a picnic, a picnic!' they chanted. Jenny rolled her eyes heavenwards.

'Oh, Findlay, *now* look what you've done!' she reproached him. 'Why can't you keep your brilliant ideas to yourself?'

He did not appear to hear her, but just went on talking. 'If I call at one o'clock tomorrow, with some bits and pieces from Marks and Spencer's food hall, could you have them ready in their scruffiest clothes? We could go somewhere for them to let rip and use up their surplus energy. Charmouth beach is nice, especially when the tide's out.'

Jenny blinked and shook her head in disbelief at what she had just heard. Or had she misunderstood?

'Excuse me, Findlay, but did you say that you'll call here tomorrow to take these children out?' she asked incredulously. 'What about your parents?'

'I shall have enough time with them, and it would be a useful way to spend an afternoon. Why, don't you think it's a good idea, Jenny?'

The children answered for her, with shouts of 'Yes, yes, yes! We like going for picnics!'

'Good!' He nodded and gave a thumbs-up sign. 'One o'clock, then. Thirteen hundred hours.'

'Zero hour and ready for blast-off,' replied Jenny dazedly.

Goodness, she thought as she waved to his disappearing car. Was he mad?

CHAPTER FIVE

SHEILA was both impressed and amused when she heard of the plan for Saturday afternoon.

'Oh, my! He must be really keen on you, Jenny—and isn't he *gorgeous*? I don't feel so guilty now about palming the kids off on you! Shall I make some Marmite and peanut butter sandwiches for them?'

'He said he'd bring the food, Sheila, but perhaps I should take something too,' said Jenny. 'And maybe spare socks and pants for them all if we're going to a beach!'

She could still hardly believe that Findlay had offered to give up a whole afternoon to entertain three children whom he did not even know. Was it *only* for Grannie's sake? Tossing and turning in an unfamiliar bed that night, Jenny relived the incredible sensation of his kiss, his mention of that someone he had loved and the tears which had sprung from some deep well of desolation.

Jenny's thoughts circled restlessly. Had he been in love with someone who had not responded—who might, in fact, have betrayed him? Surely no woman could be that mad! Or perhaps she had been married already, possibly with children—and Findlay was not the sort of man who would do anything dishonourable. Might that account for him giving up a distinguished career to go and bury himself in Brazil to devote his life to the poor and underprivileged? Jenny longed to know her name...

As she lay awake in the darkness the idea came to her

that if the past was truly past, leaving only a memory of what had been, then surely there was a chance that he could one day put it behind him and find another love—perhaps not as deep as the one he had lost, but which still might bring him happiness and lead to marriage…and children?

Jenny let her imagination picture a future in which Findlay d'Arc would choose another love to take the place of the one he had lost.

Someone like herself? Oh, Findlay—Findlay d'Arc!

And with his name on her lips she at last fell asleep.

She was as excited as the children on Saturday morning, and although Sheila's and Carol's teasing remarks about Findlay made her blush she secretly hoped that they were not entirely unfounded.

Findlay d'Arc received a clamorous greeting on his arrival.

'What's your name?' demanded Simon.

'Don't be such a rude little boy!' said Grannie severely. 'The gentleman is Dr Findlay to you.'

'How old are you, Dr Finny?'

'So old that I've lost count, Simon—how young are *you*?' countered Findlay.

'He's four and I'm six,' cut in Vicki. 'Dr Fin'lay, are you going to marry Jenny Poppins? My mummy said you might.'

Jenny blushed crimson. 'That's enough nonsense. Off you go and get into—er—Findlay's car. Hurry up!' she ordered, avoiding Findlay's eye.

When the three children were belted into the back seat Jenny took her place beside Findlay and they set off through the rolling hills and patchwork fields of Dorset, now in their full spring glory. Pink and white fruit blossom drifted like clouds amidst a myriad shades of green, and Jenny pointed out the new lambs, skipping among the flocks of sheep, and the baby calves with their mothers in the pastures.

When they reached the summit of the hill above Lyme Regis they all exclaimed at the sight of the blue sea sparkling in the sunshine.

'Look, William, there's the Cobb curving out from the shore, with all those little fishing-boats sheltering against it,' said Jenny, pointing to the ancient structure that had served as defence, landing-stage and breakwater for six hundred years.

'Can we walk along it?' asked William.

'Yes, but you must be careful not to fall off—there's no rail to hold onto!'

As soon as Findlay had parked the car they went down to the harbour and climbed the steps to the Upper Cobb. The children ran ahead to its furthest point, and Findlay took Jenny's arm as they followed at a leisurely pace.

'Did you see the film *The French Lieutenant's Woman*?' she asked him. 'It was filmed here, and I feel as if I'm walking in her footsteps.'

He smiled. 'No, I didn't see it, but I've heard the book's very good. *My* literary heroine of Lyme is Jane Austen.'

'Ah!' breathed Jenny, remembering the film she had seen with Steve. 'Did she come here?'

'Yes, and she put the Cobb into *Persuasion*, her last novel, which I think is my favourite. Do you know it?'

'No, but I'll read it as soon as I—'

They had caught up with the children who now gathered round them, all talking at once as they looked back at the shore and the town perched above it.

'Look, Jenny, the hills are trying to tip the houses into the sea!' cried Vicki.

'No, they're not, silly,' said William with a superior air.

'As a matter of fact, Vicki, something like that *did* happen about a hundred and fifty years ago,' Findlay told her. 'There was a great big storm, and a slice of the cliff slid down into the sea, taking a few houses with it. What a splash that must have been! It's how the Undercliff was formed—can you see?'

'Oh, I remember the Undercliff in the film,' said Jenny. 'It's where the French Lieutenant's woman used to go walking, and met the man who was to be her—er—'

She broke off as the children begged to walk there too.

'Too far away for your little legs,' said Findlay. 'But I'll tell you what—we'll go to the Lyme Museum and see the model of that big landslip. Come on!'

With Vicki clinging to Findlay's hand and Simon between Jenny and William, they walked up to the old town with its steep, narrow streets and found the quaint little museum where Vicki and Simon at once rushed to the central spiral staircase and clattered happily up and down, their shrill voices echoing round the building. Findlay and William studied the reconstruction of the landslip and gazed in wonder at the huge bones of pre-historic animals.

'We'd better beat it out of here before those two imps get us thrown out,' warned Jenny.

'All right! I vote for ice creams all round, and then

back to the car and off to Charmouth,' replied Findlay
to shouts of agreement.

Can this really be *me*, marvelled Jenny, strolling along
with the new obs and gynae consultant, on this lovely
day by the sea, with three children and licking an ice
cream? And I thought that my life had come to a social
dead-end at Stretbury!

The tide had been right out at Charmouth, and was
just starting to flow in again. Backed by steep and rocky
cliffs into which a flight of steps had been built, the
beach was perfect for children to play and paddle at the
edge of the little oncoming waves.

Off came sandals and socks, and Findlay rolled up his
trousers to accompany the boys, splashing happily in the
shallows, while Jenny and Vicki built a sandcastle complete with a moat. There were several other groups on
the beach, and two little boys joined William and Simon.
Their mother smiled at Jenny.

'Lovely day for the kids! Are you down here on holi-
day?'

'No, only a day trip,' answered Jenny.

'Your husband seems to be enjoying himself as much
as the boys! I left mine stuck in front of the box, watching the Cup Final,' added the young mother with a
shrug.

Jenny smiled her sympathy and hadn't the heart to
correct the mistake. Instead, she gave herself up to the
delightful fantasy of being Mrs Findlay d'Arc for an
afternoon, with a ready-made family.

Findlay looked at his watch and came over to them.

'Is it nearly picnic time?' he asked. 'Shall we open
the basket and find out what's in it?'

A chorus of 'Ooh!' and 'Ah!' greeted the selection of

savoury crisps and nibbles, jam tarts and sponge fingers, while out of an ice-cooled container he took a variety of sandwiches and tiny sausage rolls. There were fruit juices to be sipped through straws, and Jenny produced a flask of coffee for Findlay and herself.

With her own contribution of children's sandwiches, there was enough food to include the two little boys and their mother, who sat down beside Jenny and accepted their hospitality.

'You look much too young to be the mother of these three,' she remarked. 'D'you mind telling me how old you were when you got married?'

Everybody seemed to stop munching, and into the silence Vicki's little voice piped up.

'Dr Fin'lay and Jenny Poppins are only pretending to be married,' she explained. 'They're not, *really*.'

Jenny choked on her coffee, but was saved from having to reply by the arrival of an elderly gentleman who had descended the cliff steps and quietly approached them across the sand. Nobody noticed him until he laid a hand on Findlay's shoulder.

'Allo, 'allo! It is a good place to picnic, yes?' he said in a pleasantly accented voice. 'I discover that you have a secret family, Findlay! What will your mother say?'

Findlay jumped up, his face alight with pleasure.

'Papa! *Comment vas-tu, mon père*?' he cried. 'Jenny, this is my father, Henri d'Arc.'

Jenny scrambled to her feet, thankful for the diversion.

'*Bonjour, monsieur*!' she said in her best school French, taking his proffered hand.

'*Enchanté, chère mademoiselle*,' replied the old gentleman, his dark brown eyes twinkling at her under heavy lids. His skin was a warm olive colour like his son's, though finely wrinkled, and with his silver hair and short pointed beard he was like an older version of Findlay. Jenny took to him on sight.

'Papa, this is Miss Jenny Curtis, the hospital sister I told you about—and this is her young cousin William. Vicki and Simon are also related to her.'

'*Alors*! I am glad to meet you all—William—Vicki—Simon! Are you enjoying your visit to Lyme, Miss Curtis?'

'Very much—and please call me Jenny.'

'*Certainement*—if you call me Henri.' Turning to his son, he went on, 'I have been ordered to bring you home with me so that your mother may meet your guests.'

'What, *all* of us, Papa?' Findlay looked surprised.

'That is my instruction, yes,' replied his father. 'Fiona was quite firm about it. I think she wants to see what company you keep!'

His laughter reassured Jenny to some extent, but she was dismayed by the prospect of meeting Mrs d'Arc in her present dishevelled state, with sand in her hair and clothes and three distinctly grubby children in tow. She hesitated.

'I think we should be getting back to Dewsfold soon—'

'It will not take long, Jenny,' said Henri, sweeping aside any objections. 'I will return home now to tell Fiona that you will come as soon as you finish your picnic, yes?'

There was no escape, and Jenny could scarcely hide her nervousness. Was this a genuine wish of Findlay's mother to meet his friends, or curiosity to see the girl who had enticed him away from an all too brief visit home? Either way, Jenny felt at a disadvantage, and as they packed the remains of the picnic into the car boot she had a sense of foreboding.

Catching Findlay's eye, she lifted her chin and re-solved to be cool and matter-of-fact. She had never set out to impress the consultant, and now there was no chance to impress his parents: they must take her as they found her!

As they approached the elegant three-storeyed house within its high-walled garden Jenny was thankful that she had already met Findlay's father, but felt far more apprehensive about his mother. In reply to her casual questions on the drive, Findlay told her that Fiona d'Arc was Scottish by birth, and after her marriage to Henri had gone to live in France for a number of years. Findlay had been their only child.

When the tall, upright old lady appeared on the terrace to greet them Jenny felt fairly sure that her warning vibes had been justified, and some instinct warned her to be on her guard.

Mrs d'Arc wore an afternoon dress in two shades of turquoise which flattered her pale complexion and the red glints that still remained in her smoothly coiled hair. Her sea-blue eyes did not miss a thing, and even Simon was reduced to a gaping silence by her aloof expression. Jenny was struck by Findlay's resemblance to both his parents, and thought he was a perfect blend of their best points.

Mrs d'Arc offered them drinks of tea or iced mineral water, and Jenny had to explain that the children were full up after their picnic.

'Would they like to play croquet on the lawn? Even the little ones can try their skill at hitting the balls through the hoops,' suggested Mrs d'Arc. As the children had never even heard of croquet, Henri and Findlay took them to practise some simple shots with the mallets. The lawn lay below the terrace, approached by a flight of stone steps, and Jenny was left alone with her hostess.

'Would you like to see round the garden, Miss Curtis?' asked Fiona d'Arc in a tone that made it sound like an order. 'I'm growing tomatoes and courgettes in the greenhouse to make my own ratatouille. Are you a gardener, Miss Curtis?'

Jenny was careful to say 'Mrs d'Arc' as she replied that she was interested but did not get much time for it.

'Ah, yes, I hear that you work with Findlay in the operating theatre,' remarked the older woman as they walked along a paved path between several varieties of herbs.

'Yes, we make quite a good team, together with the anaesthetist and other theatre staff,' replied Jenny carefully.

'Are you a midwife, Miss Curtis?'

'Yes, but I haven't much post-graduate experience in it, Mrs d'Arc—I'm more into theatre and surgical nursing.'

'Have you ever worked abroad?'

'No, not so far.' What's all this leading up to? she wondered.

'During his time in Brazil my son worked under conditions you could hardly imagine, Miss Curtis, and brought his expertise to the service of poor women who could never have paid for a specialist of his calibre. Obstetrics is much more advanced now than when he was born forty-two years ago when I nearly died.

'I've often wondered if that influenced him in his choice of speciality because I know what deep satisfaction it gives him to ease the lives—and, in fact, sometimes *save* the lives—of women from every walk of life. That is my son's relationship with the female sex, Miss Curtis, and is a purely professional one.'

Jenny felt somewhat bewildered.

'Do you mean that he isn't interested in any other kind of relationship with them? I mean, with a woman?' she asked rather confusedly.

'Not now. Not after Gabriella. Their marriage was brief but very special, Miss Curtis, and has had a lasting effect upon his life.'

Jenny's heart lurched wildly, and she stopped in her tracks. *Gabriella*—so that was her name. And *marriage*?

Mrs d'Arc also stood still and faced Jenny as she continued speaking in a cool and level tone. 'Since the death of our dear daughter-in-law my son's life has been dedicated to the service of women through his work, whether in Edinburgh, Paris, Bristol or some remote part of the Third World, Miss Curtis.

'Many women have thrown themselves in his path and have been disappointed, not realising that there can be no other woman for him after Gabriella. She was unique, we all adored her and she lives on in our hearts.'

Jenny's head was spinning, and she felt that she didn't want to hear any more from this woman.

'I hardly see why you should think that this concerns *me*, Mrs d'Arc,' she said quietly.

'Good, I'm pleased to hear you say that, my dear. I would not like to think of you mistaking my son's natural cordiality for something more, as some others have done.'

Jenny gasped, and a wave of indignation swept over

her at such condescension. She was silent for a few moments, and then spoke up clearly.

'Look down there, Mrs d'Arc, and see how much
Findlay's enjoying himself, playing with those children.
Not many men would want to spend a whole afternoon
keeping them occupied and happy. It makes me think
what a wonderful father he'd make. And, be honest,
wouldn't you like to have grandchildren?'

It was Fiona d'Arc's turn to gasp at such effrontery.
She stood quite still and regarded Jenny with her cold
blue eyes.

'You don't understand as well as I thought, Miss
Curtis. My son made a definite decision to forego family
life, and dedicate himself to his profession, out of devotion to his wife's memory. He knew that she was dying when he married her, and nobody will ever take her
place. Do you understand me?'

'Yes, Mrs d'Arc, you've made yourself quite clear,'
replied Jenny steadily.

'Good. Now let me show you the rock-garden. The
aubretia has been wonderful this year.'

Jenny somehow managed to nod and make appropri-
ate comments on the flowers and vegetables, but inwardly she was shaken by the tragic story of Findlay's
marriage and also by the blatant warning-off that she had
been given by his mother. She perceived Mrs d'Arc's
jealous possessiveness towards her son, and suspected
that Gabriella's greatest asset was that she was dead.

It was a relief when the children returned with Findlay
and his father, full of their exploits at 'crokey', and of
how Simon had hit a ball right up in the air and Dr Finny
had caught it in his hand.

'It is a miracle that my spectacles are still intact,' said

Henri ruefully. 'I did not realise it was such a dangerous game!'

Jenny was thankful for the children's giggling and chatter on the drive back to Dewsfold, which meant that there was no need to say anything about her conversation with Mrs d'Arc.

Sunday was another hectic day, with the buffet lunch and Amanda's party. Jenny was put in charge of entertaining the children, including half a dozen of Amanda's classmates, and also helped Grannie to dress up in her best outfit. The old lady looked so charming and sweet that Jenny wished Grampy could see her.

The party went off well, but Grannie was very tired by the end and was thankful when Findlay appeared at five o'clock to drive them home.

'Congratulations on your looks and your stamina, Mrs Curtis,' he said with a smile as he helped her into the passenger seat, while Jenny said her goodbyes to the children. Sheila gave her a specially grateful hug.

'It's been simply wonderful having you here, Jenny, and I hope it won't be long before you come to stay with us again,' she said. 'And bring Dr Gorgeous with you!'

Jenny could not foresee another visit to Dewsfold in the near future, but it was nice to know that she'd be welcome.

Very little was said on the journey home, and Grannie fell asleep with her head on Findlay's shoulder. Jenny deliberately directed her thoughts to the following day and Mr Gould's admission to the men's ward: he would need three days of preparation for surgery. Not for the first time in her nursing career Jenny silently thanked heaven for her patients and their need of her skill and care.

It helped to take her mind off Fiona d'Arc's chilling warning: 'There can be no other woman for him after Gabriella.'

Too late, thought Jenny as she faced the truth in her heart. I've gone and fallen in love with a forbidden man.

CHAPTER SIX

As SOON as Jenny entered the men's ward on Monday morning she knew that all her attention would need to be directed there.

'We're getting three fourth-day post-ops today, two from Bristol and a Mr Sidney Horner from Gloucester, who's had a total colectomy and colostomy,' she told Staff Nurse Barnett. 'Perhaps he'll be willing to share his experience with Mr Peter Gould, who's for admission today and operation on Thursday—but we must respect their privacy and not put pressure on either of them.'

'Isn't it nice that Mr Gould is to have his op done here, Sister?' said Mavis Barnett, whose youngest child was at Stretbury Junior School. 'Will he be going into the single room?'

'No, he'd better go in the last bed on the right, next to the bay,' replied Jenny. 'I can't turn George out.'

Old George Burton had suffered a second stroke in his eighties, and his life was peacefully drawing to a close.

Mr Horner turned out to be a pale, tired-looking man in his mid-sixties, who seemed exhausted after the journey by ambulance. Jenny found that his temperature and pulse rate were both raised, and checked his wound dressing and colostomy.

'I see you've got rid of your drip and catheter, Mr Horner, and that you're on free fluids,' she said cheerfully, after consulting his case-notes. 'Fancy a cup of tea?'

'I would that, Sister, I'm parched,' he groaned. 'I'll have a couple o' them painkillers, an' all—that drive shook me up summat rotten.'

Oh, dear, thought Jenny, this poor old chap won't be much of a role model for Mr Gould! Better warn Mavis not to mention him to Peter at least until he's had a chance to settle in.

During her lunch hour she called in at the Hylton annexe to see Grampy.

'He was a bit mopy over the weekend, with his wife being away and Andrew off as well,' reported Sister Mason. 'But, taken all round, he's made marvellous strides in the last couple of weeks. It just goes to show what can be achieved by motivation and a genuine interest in some kind of activity.'

'But what about the incontinence, Winnie? Does he still have accidents?' Jenny enquired.

'Very seldom during the day. He's worked out his own timetable with that screw-top jar,' replied the sister with a shrug. 'I'd prefer him to use the toilet, of course, but he manages to stay dry, which is the main thing! At night he has plastic-backed pads and a drawsheet. With luck, we shall soon be able to start thinking about a home visit and then discharge under the care of the community staff and social services.'

'Grannie will be overjoyed,' murmured Jenny, who had hardly dared to hope for such an outcome.

Grampy's eyes brightened at the sight of her.

'Doris has been in this morning, and told me what a

houseful you had down at Dewsfold,' he said. 'I think she was glad to get home again.'

'Yes, it was a bit hectic, Grampy. Sheila's sister's two children are a pair of imps!'

'Still, it was a shame I couldn't go with you and Doris,' he said wistfully. 'She said she missed me.'

'We *both* did, Grampy,' Jenny told him, though she wondered what Vicki and Simon would have said about the screw-top jar!

Peter and Brenda Gould greeted Jenny warmly, and Peter seemed calm and hopeful when she sat down with them in the ward office with a tray of tea to outline the pre-operative regime.

'Fluids only for forty-eight hours beforehand, Peter, and I'll have to give you a colonic wash-out on Wednesday evening to make really sure that your bowel's empty,' she said apologetically. 'The physiotherapist will come to see you to start you practising some breathing and leg exercises so that you'll know what to do when we nag you after the op!'

'Is that to prevent chest infection?' asked Mrs Gould

'Yes, and also to prevent blood clots from floating around and getting lodged in the chest or the big artery in each leg. That's why we'll haul you out of bed on the day after operation—oh, we're a hard-hearted lot in here, Peter, I'm warning you!'

'Will I be able to have a smoke, Sister Curtis? Only one or two a day,' pleaded the headmaster, looking like a guilty schoolboy.

'Ah! This is a non-smoking area, and a great opportunity for you to kick the evil weed, don't you agree?' asked Jenny, but when she saw how his face fell, and remembering the three anxious days ahead, she relented a little.

'Look, Peter, if you happen to go for a stroll in the grounds I'll turn my blind eye in your direction, but don't let Dr McGuire catch you at it—he'll be giving your anaesthetic!'

As the Goulds chuckled gratefully Jenny cleared her throat before her next words.

'You'll also meet the stoma nurse, the specialist in caring for your colostomy, Peter. She'll see you before and after your op, and visit you at home to check that you're well organised. Any problems or questions— you've only got to ask, right?'

There were more points to be made about the immediate pre-operative routine procedures, but Jenny knew that her patient needed time to take in the information already given. She switched to asking about the Goulds' grown-up family, and was told that their married daughter, Olivia, had a little boy, their first grandchild and the apple of their eye. Remembering what this man had suffered at the time of the colonoscopy, Jenny now wanted to build up an atmosphere of trust and confidence.

'By the way, Peter, Mr Findlay d'Arc will be over here tomorrow for the gynae operation list. Shall I tell him that you're in?'

'Oh, *do*, Sister! I'd be glad to see him at any time he's got a moment to spare. I only met him on that one occasion, but I'll never forget what he did for me then. Never.'

Jenny's brown eyes softened, and her lips curved up in a little smile as she remembered how she had begged Findlay to try to allay this man's unspoken fear. What had she said to him?

'You look as if you've had some experience with this sort of thing, Mr d'Arc.'

Of course. Gabriella, the wife he had loved and lost so tragically soon.

Night Sister Pilgrim was speaking on the telephone in the men's ward office when Jenny arrived the following morning.

'Yes, the surgeon thinks it's a partial obstruction following his operation, Mrs Horner. It happens sometimes—the bowel just refuses to move in the usual way. No, we can't be sure yet. He's had blood samples taken to see if there's any infection, and we've started a new course of strong antibiotics. Yes, we've put him back on the drip, and the tube to keep his tummy empty. Yes, of course it's a setback, Mrs Horner, but try not to get upset, dear. Yes, of course I will. Right, then—goodbye.'

She replaced the receiver and turned to Jenny, whose face registered dismay.

'Oh, Lord! It's a funny thing, Sister Pilgrim, but I had this feeling about poor old Mr Horner yesterday—that he was cooking up something. Is it a paralytic ileus? Bit late on his fifth day, isn't it?'

'Could be one of several things,' said the night sister. 'He can't keep anything down, his temperature's way up and his pulse is racing, he's sweating—'

'Internal haemorrhage?' Jenny asked sharply.

'Don't think so—his blood pressure's not that low. Dr McGuire's been on to the surgical registrar at Gloucester, and he's coming over later this morning. Meanwhile, he said to give morphine, recommence drip-and-suction, and start cephalosporin and intravenous Flagyl. All of which we've done.'

'Heavens! And I've got this gynae list in Theatre,' lamented Jenny. 'It looks as if we're going to need that single room, after all, and transfer dear old George to the Hylton annexe—just what I didn't want to do so near to the end.'

She sighed regretfully and went to see Mr Horner. For the first time since commencing her new job at Stretbury Memorial Jenny was conscious of the weight of responsibility when nursing an acutely ill patient in a general practitioners' hospital, with no surgical or medical team immediately on hand.

It was a quarter to nine when she rushed into the theatre. Dr McGuire was also late arriving, and Findlay d'Arc and Steve Forrest had to stand around for almost ten minutes, gowned and gloved, before the first patient was wheeled in. Jenny explained the reason for the delay as she prepared her instrument trolley.

'Hmm, yes, Sister Curtis. When unforeseen complications occur they highlight a staff crisis,' observed Findlay with his usual formality in Theatre, while Steve declared that Jenny was being shamelessly exploited by the hospital NHS trust committee.

'As I see it, you do the work of two point five nursing staff, Jenny.' Lowering his tone, he asked, 'By the way, are you free tomorrow evening, darling?'

'No, I most certainly am not, Steve,' she snapped. 'I've got this patient for major surgery under Mr Jamieson on Thursday morning here—'

'Oh, is that Mr Gould?' asked Findlay, overhearing. 'I must come over and have a word with him when we've finished in here.'

He gave Jenny an encouraging smile. 'Looks like being one of those weeks, Sister Curtis! Our little weekend trip already seems a long time ago, doesn't it?'

There was a moment of complete silence in the theatre. Doreen and Jill exchanged one of their meaningful looks and Steve's open-mouthed astonishment made Jenny want to laugh out loud, but she simply acknowledged Findlay's friendly remark with a half-smile. Let them think what they like, she thought: *honi soit qui mal y pense*!

At the end of the list—while Findlay was writing up the patients' case-notes—Steve seized Jenny as she emerged from the changing-room.

'Look, when can I see you again, Jenny?' he demanded. 'All this rubbish about pressure of work! What you need is an evening out—a complete break from this place. When are you free next?'

'Not this week, Steve, honestly.'

'Next week, then—or I'll come and carry you off for your own good!'

Jenny sighed. It was impossible to explain her confused emotional state to this eager young doctor.

'It's kind of you, Steve, but right now I'm not really looking for a relationship, if you see what I mean,' she temporised, at the same time thinking that it would be a nice change to be taken out. Steve at once took the hint.

'I understand, Jenny, don't worry,' he reassured her. 'Surely you don't think I'd ever wreck my chances with you—or any girl for that matter—by not heeding the signals! All I'm asking is to let me take you somewhere nice and buy you dinner. And afterwards I'll guarantee to deliver you back to dear old Grandma, safe and sound!'

It seemed silly to refuse, and he arranged to call for her at Bailey's Cottage on the following Tuesday.

'By the way, Jenny,' he went on, 'what, may I ask, was friend Findlay on about in there? Something about a weekend trip—what did he mean?'

'Exactly what he said, Steve. He gave Grannie and me a lift to my uncle's home at Dewsfold in Somerset, and brought us back again on Sunday evening. Wasn't it kind of him?'

'What, all that distance—and each way? Good God!'

Steve was genuinely taken aback, and began to have odd suspicions regarding the other-worldly Mr d'Arc. What exactly was the motive behind all this interest in Jenny's ancient grandparents? Perhaps he ought to keep a closer watch on friend Findlay…

Jenny hurried back to the men's ward to find that the surgeon from Gloucester had been to see Mr Horner and discussed his problem with Dr McGuire. A wait-and-see policy had been adopted, with close observations and all treatment to be continued. Staff Nurse Barnett and Sister Mason had arranged the transfer of old George Burton to the Hylton annexe, and the single room was being prepared for Mr Horner.

Jenny noticed that the curtains were drawn around Mr Gould's bed, and wondered if the physiotherapist or stoma nurse was with him. On taking a peep, however, she found that his visitor was Findlay d'Arc, and that his arrival was well timed. Mr Gould was clearly upset, and in need of emotional support.

Findlay looked up at Jenny and gave her a warning wink.

'Ah, Sister Curtis! There are no secrets in a hospital ward, are there? Peter had a ringside seat when the sur-

geon came to see Mr Horner, and it's naturally made
him ask a few questions about bowel surgery and colostomy. I've been telling him that it's never wise to make
comparisons!'

Jenny's heart sank, but she put on a bright smile for
Mr Gould.

'Oh, how I agree with that, Mr d'Arc. Sidney Horner
had more extensive surgery than you'll need, Peter, and
he's also about ten years older and not in such good
shape.'

'But the poor devil looks *ghastly*, Sister—more dead
than alive when they wheeled him into that single room,'
answered Gould, totally unconvinced. 'If I look like *that*
after the op heaven help my poor wife when she comes
to see me! And all the paraphernalia—drips and drainage
tubes, especially that one up his nose—oh, my God!'

His newly found hopefulness and confidence had been
swept away at a stroke by Sidney Horner's unfortunate
setback, and nothing that Jenny or Findlay could say was
able to restore it.

'It makes me wonder if it's worthwhile, going through
with all this, Findlay,' he muttered, the tightness of his
mouth betraying his tension. 'Maybe it's just prolonging
the agony for the sake of a short reprieve from the inevitable.'

'Oh, come off it, Peter, you're not going to back out
now,' urged Findlay. 'With so many people cheering for
you—your wife and family, your school pupils and staff,
everybody here—all these good wishes, thoughts and
prayers—'

'They'd better not look to me for an example of courage, Findlay. I could let them all down.' Peter Gould's
voice shook, and they each desperately tried to think of

something to encourage this frightened man. Jenny suddenly remembered his grandson.

'Did you say your eldest daughter has a little boy?' she asked on an impulse.

'Yes, our first grandchild. His name's Philip, and he'll be two in July,' sighed Peter Gould, though his tense features softened a little at the thought of this much-loved latest member of the family.

'And where does your daughter live?' asked Jenny with a quick nod at Findlay.

'Stroud. Olivia and her husband are coming to visit this evening,' Peter Gould told them. 'She has a friend who'll babysit.'

'Right!' Findlay was in no doubt about the next move. 'Get Olivia to bring Philip in this afternoon—the sooner the better.'

'But her husband's got the car at work—'

'Then ring her up and ask her to come on the bus— or bring Philip in with them this evening. One late night won't matter. You need to be reminded of how much you've got to live for, old chap. A little grandson— ah-h!'

There was a depth of feeling in the murmuring sigh that he gave, and Jenny reflected that he had no children himself—nor was he likely to, if what his mother had said was true.

'Brilliant!' she exclaimed. 'Look, couldn't your wife get in touch with Olivia, and fetch her and Philip in your car? I'll bring you the trolley-phone, and you can get it arranged. Doctor's orders, tell her!'

Peter Gould's face brightened as Findlay rose from the bedside, giving Jenny a discreet thumbs-up sign. She replied with a melodramatic upward roll of her eyes as she went off in search of the mobile telephone. How had Findlay *known*, she wondered, how best to give Peter the necessary incentive to face the coming ordeal?

And, indeed, when Philip arrived that afternoon with his mother and grandmother he charmed the whole ward, toddling on his fat little legs to 'Gan-dad' and holding out his arms for a hug. Jenny saw the expression on Peter Gould's face as he held the child close, and blinked away a glimmer of tears.

In the ward office Mrs Gould asked Jenny about the condition of Mr Horner, and his prospects of recovery.

'I'm really sorry about this bit of bad timing, Brenda,' said Jenny. 'In answer to your question, let me put it this way: if I were a betting woman, I'd lay you five pounds to a penny that this time next week your husband and Sidney Horner will be sitting over there in those two armchairs by the bay window, telling each other how they came through against all odds and capping each other's stories. Just you wait and see!'

'I'm sorry, Sister Garrett, but there's no way I can help out at the antenatal clinic this afternoon. I've got sick patients to care for, and they come first.'

Jenny was adamant. After a morning spent in the theatre, assisting Mr Jamieson and his registrar to remove an annular carcinoma of the sigmoid colon, and the formation of an external opening—a colostomy—on Mr Gould, with Conor McGuire as anaesthetist, she intended to devote the rest of her day on duty to caring for this patient in his first post-operative phase.

Sister Barr had sent a nursing auxiliary from the women's ward to help with the routine work and Jenny had two staff nurses on duty, but all hands were needed as Sidney Horner's condition was only slowly respond-ing to treatment and he still needed vigilant nursing care.

Wendy Garrett complained that she had not been told of the situation, and was relying on Jenny's assistance at the busy Thursday clinic.

'Sister McGuire always managed to delegate the available staff so as to be free on clinic days,' she de-clared. 'A little more foresight and forward planning is all that's needed.'

Jenny saw red, and no longer felt obliged to be apolo-getic.

'Well, here's a bit of foresight for you, Sister Garrett,' she retorted. 'Your paragon of virtue, Mrs McGuire, is due at the clinic this afternoon for her thirty-four-week check so why not get *her* to chaperon Mr d'Arc? Quite frankly, the clinic is the last thing on my mind right now!'

The midwife flounced off, and Jenny returned to Peter Gould's bedside.

'Hello, Peter, hello. You're back in the ward again, and everything's fine,' she said softly. 'Can you hear me, Peter? It's all over, and you're doing really well.'

He moaned and moved his head on the pillow as she wiped his mouth with a gauze square dipped in iced water. She repeated his name several times until she got a whispered reply, 'Hello, Sister.' His temperature, pulse and blood pressure were recorded half-hourly, and by mid-afternoon Jenny asked the auxiliary to help her sit him up on a bank of pillows. She gave him a pain-relieving injection, after which he slept undisturbed for two hours.

Jenny went to attend to Sidney Horner, now notice-ably recovering from the partial obstruction at the site of operation, where internal bruising and swelling had not been helped by too-early discontinuation of the drip-and-suction post-operative regime. He smiled faintly at Jenny, and said he felt hungry for the first time.

'Me poor ol' tum's rumbling around like a thunder-storm, Sister.'

'Thank heaven for that, Sidney!' she replied in heart-felt tones. Post-operative bowel sounds are sweet music in the ears of nurses, especially in abdominal surgery.

At five o'clock Jenny felt that the men's ward could be left in the care of the part-time sister who was taking the evening shift. She felt reasonably satisfied with the way that the day had gone, but now that the tension had eased she felt a sense of anticlimax, not to mention a headache and a return of the nagging stab of pain in her tummy.

She longed for her room at Bailey's Cottage, with the curtains drawn and a cool compress on her forehead, but she had to call on Grampy and so set out towards the Hylton annexe.

'Sister Curtis! Jenny! I'm so glad you're still here!'

On hearing that voice, Jenny's headache and tiredness seemed to disappear as if by magic. She turned to Findlay with an involuntary exclamation of relief at the sight of the man who had proved to be so kind and so wise in his assessment of Peter Gould, and of Grampy—and of herself.

'Goodness, the clinic must have finished an hour ago,' she said as he caught up with her.

'Actually, it went on for longer this afternoon, and there were a fair number of mothers with problems,' he told her.

'Oh, Findlay, I'm sorry I wasn't able to help out to-day.'

'Well, of course not, Jenny—but, don't worry, I had a very efficient chaperon. She had an answer for all of them. In fact, she gave out so much good advice that I felt quite superfluous!' He grinned broadly as he spoke, and Jenny stared.

'Goodness! You don't mean—not Mrs McGuire?' she gasped, and when he nodded she clapped a hand to her mouth. 'So Sister Garrett took me at my word, then?'

'Actually, Anne offered to do it, and loved every minute. In fact, she was in her element. Conor had told her about Peter's op and Sidney's collapse, and she rattled on about the staff crisis and said she'd speak to Lady Hylton. I left her deep in conversation with Dr Sellars. Anyway, how have *you* survived, little Jenny? And the men in your life—Peter and Sidney?'

She chuckled, and gave him the latest news. They were approaching the annexe, but he gently took her arm and steered her on a circuitous course around the perimeter of the grounds.

'Jenny, dear, there's something I want to say to you.'

Jenny's headache might have vanished but she now had a problem with her legs, which had suddenly turned to water.

'I did so enjoy our time with the children last Saturday, Jenny, but all the time I was thinking that I owed you an apology—or at least an explanation.'

'What for? I thought I owed *you* one for putting up with us, and for all your generosity,' she said lightly. 'That was some picnic!'

'It was nothing, Jenny. I loved it, especially your company—and after I'd behaved so stupidly with you. But you were so sweet, and seemed to understand somehow.'

He hesitated, as if not sure how to continue, and Jenny prompted him gently.

'You mean when we were beside that rhododendron bush, and you said it was nothing to do with me—that it was…someone else you were remembering?'

'Yes, that was the occasion, when I—when I should have given you some explanation…' Again he hesitated.

'Oh, Findlay, forget it! There's no need for explanations between friends!' she told him, and made a big effort to keep her voice steady as she continued, 'As a matter of fact, I *do* understand. You were remembering your wife.'

He drew a sharp intake of breath. 'So! It must have been my mother who mentioned her to you.'

'Yes, Findlay, she did. I gather that she—your wife—was French.'

'No, Italian.' He took her hand. 'Ah, Jenny, Jenny, I wanted to tell you, I really did, only I felt I shouldn't burden you with my past life. I hope that my mother didn't go on too much. She thought the world of her, you see.'

'Yes, I gathered as much,' Jenny said quietly. 'And I realise that Gabriella must have been very special and, of course, you were devastated when she—when you lost her. Tell me, Findlay, how long were you married?'

'Seven weeks.'

'Oh, Findlay, dear.' She took his hand and entwined her fingers with his in a wordless gesture.

'I've discovered that life goes on, Jenny,' he said steadily. 'And I have my work. There are always my patients needing me—and that's another good reason for keeping going.'

'Yes, that's more or less what your mother said, too.'

'What exactly *did* my mother say, Jenny, if you don't mind telling me?'

'Well, among other things, she said that there can never be another woman in your life, not like your wife.'

He smiled and sighed. 'Poor Mother, she worshipped Gabriella. Everybody did. She was such a charming and accomplished actress.'

'Actress? What, in films?' asked Jenny in surprise.

'Yes, she was Gabriella Rasi, quite a name in Italy. Her films sometimes turn up on television with English subtitles. Didn't my mother mention her career?'

'No, I rather thought she might have been a patient of yours, Findlay,' floundered Jenny, a little embarrassed.

'Oh, no. I met her while I was doing a registrar obs and gynae job in Padua. That was her home town, and she was filming there at the time. Ah, what a summer that was!'

He smiled and closed his eyes at the recollection of that other time, but Jenny was increasingly mystified.

'If you were still a registrar when you met her, Findlay, it must have been some years ago, and yet you were only married for seven weeks— Oh, I'm sorry, I shouldn't ask. It's nothing to do with me, and it must be so painful for you. Forgive me, forget what I said.'

'Jenny.'

Findlay stopped walking, and stood looking straight at her. She faced him on the path, mesmerised by those two deep, sea-blue pools that commanded her total attention.

'It's true that we were only married for those few weeks, Jenny, but we were lovers for five years.'

'Oh!' What further revelation was this? She held her breath.

'Yes, I wanted to marry her, of course, but—well, we lived in such completely different worlds, Jenny. Her acting was everything to her. It always came first and, of course, I had my work. I'd built up quite a lucrative practice in Paris, and she had a flat in Rome. We had what is known as an arrangement, you could say. Many men loved Gabriella, but she always came back to me, and I was always there for her. Only, of course, there were no children—how could there be?'

'So what happened?' she whispered.

'Leukaemia happened, Jenny.' His voice tightened. 'We were in Venice, staying on the Lido, when the lab report was phoned through. It was acute lymphoblastic leukaemia, quite advanced. And that was the day she accepted me. She was thirty-two.'

'Oh, my God.' Jenny was trembling. 'So you were married when her career finished.'

'Yes, and I was at her side to the end.'

Jenny realised that they were still holding hands.

'Thank you for telling me about her.' Inwardly she knew that it made not the slightest difference to her own feelings, but she now had a very real insight into his pain and loss.

'And thank you, too, Jenny. My mother doesn't actually know all that I've told you. She thinks of Gabriella as some sort of saint, and I've never felt I need tell her the whole story.'

'I understand that too,' answered Jenny. 'You loved her the way she was, and that's all that matters.'

She felt his lips touch her forehead very lightly as he let go of her hand.

'It's made such a difference, knowing you and talking to you. I've been living in the past for so long, and— But I'm being selfish when you've had such a demanding day. Come on, we've got to see Grampy and enquire about the progress of the tomatoes!'

Tucking her hand under his arm, he steered her towards the hospital greenhouse and its flourishing crop of seedling flowers and vegetables.

That night Jenny pondered long and deeply on what she now knew about Findlay d'Arc. There was no doubt that he valued her friendship and the real affection that had sprung up between them, a mutual understanding and trust in both their professional and personal relationship.

But his mother had been right in one respect at least.

There would never be another Gabriella. How could there be?

CHAPTER SEVEN

STEVE FORREST could not have been more attentive or considerate. He brought flowers for Grannie, and enquired about her husband's progress while Jenny put the finishing touches to her make-up. Then he drove her to a small country restaurant, known for its traditional English farmhouse fare. Tables had to be booked in advance, and Steve led Jenny to a secluded corner.

'So, Jenny, how are things at SMH?' he asked with a smile. 'How's your VIP—the one who had the big op last Thursday?'

'Peter Gould? Couldn't be better,' she replied eagerly. 'He had his wound drain out this morning, so that's the last of the tubes gone! He's taking a light diet and really enjoying it. It's a funny thing, but last week I made a bet with his wife that he and poor old Mr Horner would be sitting side by side today, capping each other's stories.'

Steve was amused. 'And did you win your bet?'

'Y-e-s, more or less. Mr Gould has been listening to Sidney's horror stories, and doing a great job of counselling! Honestly, Steve, he's a marvel for sixth day post-op, and so *good* for Sidney who's twelfth day and perking up at last—oh!'

She broke off as she saw four people being shown to the last empty table—Dr Sellars and his wife, accompanied by Lady Margaret Hylton who was escorted by Findlay d'Arc. He made sure that she was comfortably

119

seated, before taking his place opposite her. This meant that he was directly facing Jenny, and saw her look of surprised recognition. He smiled, but she could not entirely hide her vexation at being discovered dining with Steve.

'Of all the restaurants they could have chosen, why did they have to pick this one?' she muttered across the table.

'What does it matter, Jenny? Just one of those coincidences,' Steve replied unconcernedly. He was, in fact, delighted that Findlay d'Arc should see him in an intimate tête-à-tête with Jenny.

Jenny could hardly get up and go over to tell Findlay that she was not seriously involved with his houseman, but her eyes kept meeting his and hastily looking away. Once again her appetite deserted her, and she took only small helpings of new potatoes, broccoli and fresh asparagus with her lamb cutlets.

'Jenny, darling, you're not eating enough to keep a bird alive,' commented Steve.

'I'm all right, Steve, honestly.' She made an effort to smile, and sipped a little water.

'That place isn't doing you any good, Jenny. I've watched you lose weight and go down and down. Frankly, I'm not happy about you. You're exploited.'

'Oh, do shut up, Steve. It's nothing to do with work.' Jenny's voice had an edge.

'Then what is it, for God's sake? Look, I care about you, and I—'

He broke off as the substantial shadow of Lady Hylton loomed above them. She had left her table to speak to Jenny.

'Don't get up, Miss Curtis.' The lady's magisterial

tones echoed round the dining-room. 'I want to let you know what Dr Sellars and I have been discussing. Last week dear Mrs McGuire spoke to me about the staff crisis—did you know that she actually had to assist at the antenatal clinic?

'Although I'm delighted that Mr Jamieson's decided to do the odd endoscopy and even an occasional major operation at our hospital, I do realise what an extra strain it puts on an already depleted staff.'

All Jenny realised was that they were the focus of attention of the other diners.

'I understand what you say, Lady Hylton, but I'm sure—'

'Mr d'Arc is in full agreement that there's only one course to take, Miss Curtis. We urgently need at least two more trained staff to tide us over until the new senior nursing officer arrives in September. There is no time to advertise. We need help *now* and so I have decided, rather against my stated principles, to apply to a nursing agency.'

'If you feel it's necessary, Lady Hylton ' began Jenny.

'Well, I think it's a step in the right direction,' interposed Steve. 'I must admit I've been worried about Jenny ever since she took up this new post.'

'No need to worry further, Dr—er— Help is at hand.' Lady Hylton beamed. 'That's why I'm letting your friend, Miss Curtis, know straight away about the decision.'

'And letting everybody else in this restaurant know, too,' grinned Steve when the lady had returned to her table. 'I ask you, what a way to run a hospital!'

'I'd rather deal with Lady Maggie than *some* managers I could name,' Jenny answered sharply. 'At least nobody can call her methods underhand!'

She was again aware of Findlay's eyes resting on her, but did not see the look that Steve sent in his direction from time to time—the assured, complacent look of a man who has first claim.

The days passed rapidly, and spring advanced into summer, bringing the roses into bloom on either side of the drive. Will Curtis could be seen daily at work in the greenhouse, carefully staking and tying his tomato plants as they climbed ever higher behind the sun-warmed glass, and showing Andrew how to pinch out the side-shoots that appeared between the leaf-stalks and the main stems.

The boy cheerfully climbed the stepladder to put up the hanging-baskets that Will had planted with trailing fuchsia, pansies and lobelia for the verandah of the annexe.

As Lady Margaret had promised, two new nurses appeared at the end of May. One was Heather Hulland, a big, strong Australian girl who wore her flaxen hair in a ponytail and had the kind of easy, informal manners that made Lady Hylton wince a little.

'I'm working my way around the world, ma'am, and when the agency told me about this little old place in the middle of the English country scene I reckoned I could do worse for a coupla months. At least I don't have to twist my tongue round a foreign language here!'

The other newcomer was plump, smiling Sister Absalom from Barbados, who was waiting for her husband to join her and needed temporary work for the summer. She was well experienced, and able to take charge of the women's ward, freeing Sister Barr for administrative duties. Jenny was awarded Heather, and soon realised that she had got a treasure—the men liked her easygoing manner, and she was not averse to hard work.

Peter Gould was discharged home on the fifteenth day after his operation, fully confident that he could deal with his colostomy which, it was hoped, would be closed in six to twelve months, depending on no recurrence of malignancy. Jenny was overwhelmed by the gift of a handsome dinner and tea service from him and his wife.

'I picture you using it in your home when you're Mrs You-know-who,' teased Brenda, kissing her affectionately. 'Peter and I will never be able to thank you enough for all you've done—in every way, Sister.'

Jenny was touched, of course, and said she would always treasure the set, but she was too shy to ask which you-know-who they had in mind, especially as she was obviously meant to know!

Sidney Horner's progress was slower, and he went home on his twenty-first day with a permanent colostomy. His wife gave Jenny a hand-knitted tea-cosy, and Jenny's tender heart went out to the worried woman who would have a semi-invalid to care for as they both approached their seventies. She made sure that Social Services were requested to call on the Horners to assess what additional help would be needed in the home.

And, of course, there were always Tuesday mornings and Thursday afternoons to look forward to, when Findlay d'Arc arrived to take the gynae list or the antenatal clinic with his somewhat formal, though friendly good humour. He heard Jenny's news of Grampy's home visit, which had been a great success, and had a talk with him on the day before his final discharge.

'So it's up to you, Will, old chap, and nobody else,' Findlay said seriously. 'You've done very well in the Hylton annexe, but you'll have to keep up the good work when you get home. To be honest with you, I'm just a bit worried about Doris.'

'Doris? Oh, I shan't be any trouble to her, Doctor,' replied Grampy, all smiles.

'Ah, but there's more to it than just not being any trouble, Will. You'll have to take care of her,' Findlay emphasised. 'You've got responsibilities towards her, can't you see that? She mustn't be allowed to fall back into the bad old habit of waiting on you hand and foot. From now on you contribute to the housework on a fifty-fifty basis, especially when the weather's bad and you can't do much outside.'

'Oh-ah, I see what you mean, Doctor.' The old man's eyes grew thoughtful. 'Leave it to me. I'll look after her and see she don't wear herself out again.'

'Good man. Always remember that if you want to stay in your own home you've got to prove that you're responsible enough to take control of your life. And I'm pretty sure that you are, Will, so don't let me down!'

He gave the old man a light clap on the shoulder, and thought of the additional responsibilities that Jenny would have. A home help and weekly bath-nurse had been arranged, for Jenny was not counted as a carer because of being in full-time employment. Of course, she would supervise Grampy's continuing rehabilitation, and keep a close watch for any signs of mental deterioration.

Jenny sighed as she contemplated the future, as far as she could see it. Her life was satisfying but very demanding, and she found herself looking forward to the midsummer eve party in the medical quarters of the

Bristol teaching hospital where Steve Forrest was obs and gynae houseman on Findlay d'Arc's team.

The party was fixed for the Saturday before midsummer, and Jenny had arranged to spend that night at the flat of a couple of friends, June and Freddie, to avoid arriving home late and disturbing her grandparents.

Wondering what to wear, she was delighted to find the dress of her dreams in a charity shop—a high-waisted Empire-style gown in pale green with a gauzy overskirt. She had it cleaned and, with the money saved by such a bargain, made an appointment with a top-class hairdresser to have her hair softly layered so that it resembled a smooth dark cap with curling tendrils at the nape.

Grannie and Grampy said she looked a picture, and Steve Forrest whistled when he saw her standing in the hall of Bailey's Cottage.

'Whew! You look absolutely ravishing!' he told her in frank admiration, which made Grannie look worried and Grampy none too pleased.

'Don't worry, and don't wait up, I'm staying overnight with June Masters,' she told them for the twentieth time.

'Mind you take good care of her, Doctor,' said Grampy sternly.

'I won't let her out of my sight,' grinned Steve, which did little to reassure the old couple, who came out to wave goodbye and watch the car disappear into the golden evening.

The communal lounge in the doctors' quarters had been extended, by pulling back a sliding partition to its fullest extent, which made a much larger area available for dancing. A bar at one end did a brisk trade, and a guitar group with a pianist and clarinettist supplied music to mingle with the eager voices of men and girls and the sound of laughter that rose on the summer air.

Guests stood around in chattering groups, drifting in and out of the open doors to wander outside in the walled patio and stroll along gravelled walks between flower-beds.

Jenny was soon surrounded by old friends, who exclaimed with delight at seeing her. She was kissed and embraced on all sides. Her cheeks glowed as she caught up on all the news, such as the hasty engagement of June and Freddie who were to be married as soon as Freddie got his exam results.

'And they'd better be good, Jenny, because he's going to need a job,' June confided. 'The baby's due in January, and his parents are livid. I'm sure that's why I'm feeling so yucky these days—morning *and* evening sickness!'

'Oh, you poor love,' murmured Jenny, concerned at her friend's anxious, dark-ringed eyes. 'Look, June, I won't come to the flat tonight. I'll ask Steve to drive me home. No, honestly, you need all the rest you can get—I'll be OK, don't worry.'

A worried-looking Freddie took June home soon after ten, and when she had said goodbye to them Jenny stood beside the buffet with a plate of salad and reflected on the changes in the lives of the nurse friends she had known from training days. A deep voice behind her made her start suddenly, and sent her thoughts whirling.

'How lovely you look, Jenny—straight out of Jane Austen!'

'Findlay! I—er—didn't know you'd be here,' she

stammered confusedly, thrilled by his compliment but at a loss for the right response to it.

Steve rejoined her with two iced lagers.

'Can I get you a drink, sir?' he asked.

'No, thank you, Dr Forrest. I shan't be staying long. Dr Rowland and I thought we'd look in on the midsummer revels,' answered the consultant with a smile at his companion, Diana Rowland. She was wearing her white coat over a blue checked dress, and her un-made-up face had an innocent attractiveness.

'I'm on call so it really is only a look-in.' She smiled shyly. 'You look simply gorgeous, Sister Curtis. No, thanks, Steve—oh, yes, all right, then, an orange juice. Thanks!'

'Are you busy on Maternity tonight?' Jenny asked her.

'Yes, three in labour and a possible Caesarean section. And there's been a simply awful case this evening,' she added, lowering her voice. 'This poor girl was admitted through A and E, and sent up to female surgical as acute appendicitis—but, my dear, she turned out to have a ruptured ectopic and collapsed just before she got to Theatre.

'I've never seen such a fearful haemorrhage—that's why Mr d'Arc was called in. He was furious about the delay.' She shuddered. 'Poor girl, it was touch and go.'

Jenny could not help liking this young woman and, knowing that Diana intended to work in the underdeveloped Third World after qualifying, she had to admit to herself that such a girl was just the type that Findlay might choose as a second wife and professional partner—as different from Gabriella as a woman could be. Jenny suppressed a sigh at the thought.

'Come on, darling, let's dance!' Steve was in no mood

for talking shop, and whirled Jenny off in boisterous high spirits. It was clear that he was well over the limit for driving her back to Stretbury and she thought of calling a taxi, but it seemed there was at least an hour's wait due to a huge demand.

'No problem, Jenny. Have my room and I'll kip down on a chair,' offered Steve hopefully.

No way, thought Jenny, wondering if there was an unoccupied room in the nurses' quarters.

When Diana Rowland's bleeper summoned her back to Maternity she spoke quietly to Jenny.

'Look, here's my room key. Do feel free to use it, Sister Curtis. It's going to be a busy night, and Mr d'Arc says he'll stay on for the Caesarean so I'll be assisting.'

'But suppose you get the chance of a few hours' sleep?' protested Jenny.

'I'll lie down in the nurses' rest room. I've done it before,' said Diana in her self-effacing way. 'It's quite handy when I'm likely to be called back at any minute.'

Jenny was both relieved and grateful, and at half past one she left the party and went up to Diana's room, even though Steve pleaded that it was much too early. By now she had had enough of his noisy exuberance, and was happy to escape.

She undressed and put on the nightie she had brought with her. Taking Diana's dressing-gown off the back of the door, she stood by the window and looked out at the silvery night sky and the outline of the city of Bristol. Nearer at hand she could see the lights of the maternity unit, and noted that Findlay's car was still in the park below. Oh, how she wished she was in the maternity theatre at this moment, assisting him with the Caesarean birth!

Her head throbbed slightly, and she decided to go downstairs to make a cup of tea in the small kitchen on the ground floor. On the bottom corridor she almost bumped into Steve, who was in his bathrobe. His feet were bare.

'Oh, hello. I thought you wanted to go on partying, Steve.'

'Not without you, Jenny.' He slipped his arm around her waist, giving her ribs a little tickle. 'God, you're adorable. Enough to weaken the resolution of a saint!'

She drew herself away with a smile. 'Now, then! Remember what you promised Grannie and Grampy.'

'Yes, I told them I wouldn't let you out of my sight, didn't I?' he murmured, kissing her temple and putting both arms around her so that she felt the closeness of their bodies, separated only by a couple of layers of thin material. 'Mmm!'

'Steve, it's time to say goodnight. Let me go, please.'

'Don't be cruel, darling Jenny,' he said thickly, burying his face against her neck. 'Don't you know the night was made for loving?'

'Stop it, Steve, there's somebody at the door!'

A dark shadow had appeared at the plate-glass entrance to the quarters, tapping out the code number on the silent digital lock. By the time Steve raised his head the door had swung back and the couple stared at the tall figure on the threshold. Jenny's mouth dropped open in blank dismay. Steve grinned and tightened his arms around her.

'Oh. I see. My apologies, Miss Curtis.' Findlay's tone was ice cold.

'*Findlay!*' she breathed.

'I'm sorry, I must have misunderstood Dr Rowland. I

thought she said you were in need of a lift to Stretbury. I beg your pardon for intruding. Goodnight.'

'Findlay, no! It isn't—wait!'

'He's gone, Jenny. Let him go,' said Steve, amused. 'Who cares what he thinks, anyway?'

The brief confrontation had confirmed his suspicion that the po-faced consultant fancied Jenny—the girl Steve himself had made up his mind to marry.

However, he was quite unprepared for her reaction.

'I care a great deal, as it happens! How *dare* you give him the impression that we were—were about to go to—to bed?'

Her face was dark with rage, and her eyes bright with tears of sheer vexation. To Steve she looked utterly desirable.

'Me? I didn't say a word! Though, as a matter of fact, that sounds like a pretty good idea to me—what you suggested we could do. Oh, darling—'

The stinging impact of Jenny's palm took him unawares, landing forcefully if inaccurately on the side of his nose with a painful crack. He grunted and staggered backwards as blood spurted from his left nostril, but Jenny did not wait to see the effect of her fury. She ran to the staircase and pounded up to Diana's room where she locked the door and burst into angry tears.

What had she done? How had it happened that she had lost the respect of the man she truly cared for, whose good opinion meant everything to her? Why, oh, *why* had she let herself be caught in such a compromising situation?

'Findlay—Findlay d'Arc!' Jenny sobbed into the darkness of a night that had lost its magic. She wanted nothing now but the earliest available taxi to take her home.

On the following Tuesday morning the gynae op list was conducted in the usual formal way, with little being said apart from the necessary requests and remarks as the operations were performed. It was Findlay's usual way of working so seemed no different to the rest of the team, but Jenny was aware of his coolness and he scarcely looked at Steve at all.

Jill asked the houseman innocently if he'd run into a door because of the bruise that showed faintly beneath his left eye. She got no reply but a surly shake of his head.

With Grampy now home again, there was no excuse for Findlay to visit the Hylton annexe, and at the end of the list he thanked Jenny and the two nurses for their help, and went straight to the dining-room with Conor McGuire. The GP was anxious about his wife who was having a fair amount of discomfort which disturbed her sleep, as did her frequent visits to the toilet. She was determined to go into labour naturally, but Conor was concerned that the baby's head was still high.

'Trust her to give me somethin' to worry about,' he grumbled. 'Sure and I thought it was all goin' too smoothly to be true.'

'It's probably of no significance whatever, Conor,' said the consultant, amused at the good-natured Irishman's way of expressing his fears for his adored wife, now almost due to bear their first child. 'Occipito-posterior position is the likeliest cause of an unengaged head at term in a primigravida.'

'And it's a long labour that she'll be havin', in that

case,' muttered Conor. 'How in God's name am I to endure seein' her in agony hour after hour?'

Findlay threw an arm around his shoulder. 'I won't let that happen. Courage, Conor, I've never lost a father yet!'

But he had no smiles for Jenny. It seemed as if he had withdrawn his friendship from a girl so obviously committed to another man. The pain that this caused her was even worse than the persistently grumbling appendix that now appeared to be flaring up again and made her irritable when Steve tried to draw her aside after the list.

'Jenny, I'm sorry. Please listen, will you?'

She shook off his arm and turned away abruptly. 'Excuse me, Dr Forrest, I'm needed on my ward.'

'But Jenny—'

'Good afternoon, Dr Forrest.'

There was a finality in her tone that even he could not fail to register. Watching her retreating back, he faced the fact that his romantic fling with Jenny Curtis was over beyond any doubt. He could only take consolation from the thought that friend Findlay had not witnessed his dismissal.

'Would you like to lend a hand with the antenatal clinic this afternoon, Heather?' asked Jenny on Thursday. 'Sister Garrett expects us to send somebody to help with the forty or so mums who come here to see the consultant. Most of them are booked for his delivery unit at Bristol. It's quite interesting.'

'Great! I'm not particularly up to date on obstetrics, but I'll have a go,' answered the cheerful Australian girl.

'Are you OK for taking blood samples?'

'I'm a regular little vampire, sweetie.'

'Good, you'll do for Sister Garrett, then. I wouldn't mind skipping that howling mob today,' said Jenny with a slight tightening of her mouth, which Heather noted.

'Excuse me mentioning it, sweetie, but are you feeling a bit off colour? Wrong time of the month or something?'

'Oh, no, I'm fine, just a bit tired, maybe,' Jenny replied with a shrug. 'My grandparents fuss over me quite enough, Heather, so don't you start!'

'I reckon you ought to take a bit more care,' said the other girl, eyeing her thoughtfully.

Jenny forced a smile. She knew that she really should go to see Dr Sellars and tell him about her problem, but this would mean being sent for a surgeon's opinion and a whole battery of tests, ending almost certainly with an appendicectomy. Up until now she had coped with the intermittent pain and digestive symptoms, but with the arrival of Heather and the other new sister she began to consider getting advice and treatment.

But perhaps she could still leave it for another week or two...

'Wow! He's really something, that obs and gynae bloke,' said Heather with a grin on her return from the clinic. 'Just imagine being married to something like that, oh, my! Some women get all the luck, don't they?'

'Actually he's a widower, Heather,' Jenny told her seriously.

'You don't say! That's tough for him, but it means he's back on the market and I can dream, can't I? Hey, maybe it was all in the stars that I should take this job and meet this beautiful Mr What's-his-name—what d'you think?'

'Oh, Heather!' Jenny could not repress a smile. 'Things aren't always what they seem, you know.'

'How d'you mean, sweetie?'

'Well…' Jenny hesitated as a little imp of mischief got the better of her judgement. 'Well, for a start, the second Mrs d'Arc will have to compete with the ghost of the first one and, not only that, she'll get the mother-in-law from hell.'

The Australian girl laughed out loud. 'You know something, Sister Curtis? To hear you talk, I'd almost think you'd taken a pot-shot at him yourself.'

To her annoyance, Jenny blushed. It was time for a change of subject.

'Did you notice a Mrs Anne McGuire there today?' she enquired.

'Yes, that's the other thing I meant to mention,' replied Heather. 'She's the wife of that nice Irish bloke, isn't she? The beautiful Mr d'Arc reckons she's due, and wants her in his unit this evening to get her started off with a prostaglandin pessary. Hubby couldn't wait to drag her off to pack her bags and hightail it to Bristol.'

'Hmm, she won't be very pleased,' observed Jenny.

'Well, pleased or not, she's for induction. Now come on, sweetie, get your backside out of here and off to the old folks at home!'

Jenny smiled. Heather was a very welcome addition to Stretbury Memorial.

She was just cycling out of the gate when a car turned in, the tyres skidding on the drive. It missed Jenny by a couple of inches as it zoomed past her. She wobbled violently and dismounted.

'Stupid idiot! You could have run me down!' she shouted after the driver. Then she saw that it was Conor McGuire's car. He stopped at the front entrance and leapt out; he was like a man demented.

'Help me, Sister Curtis, for the love o' God. She's on the back seat, her membranes have ruptured and the cord's comin' down. Get a stretcher, get her into Theatre now—*now*!'

Jenny left her bicycle on the grass verge and ran towards the car.

'Stop that shouting at once, Dr McGuire—*at once*!' she ordered. 'Go and fetch Sister Garrett, and bring out the stretcher trolley. I'll deal with Anne.'

He rushed off, and Jenny opened the back door of the car. Anne lay on the seat, a pillow under her bottom. She was flushed and trembling.

'Jenny, thank God you're here. My waters have broken, and when Conor examined me he felt a loop of cord through the cervix. I told him to soak a couple of tampons in warm saline to put in the vagina, then get me here as fast as he could.'

Jenny smiled reassuringly, though her heart sank. A prolapsed umbilical cord needed immediate Caesarean section if the baby's vital oxygen supply was not to be cut off.

'All right, Anne, dear, we'll get you to the theatre straight away and recall Mr d'Arc,' she said reassuringly. 'Ah, here comes the trolley.'

'Bless you, Jenny,' whispered the frightened woman, now stripped of all her former self-confidence. 'I'm so thankful that you're here to look after us.'

Jenny forgot everything else but the need to keep calm and in control of this emergency. The next twenty minutes passed like a dream in which she and Conor lifted Anne out of the car and onto the trolley, which they wheeled to the little room adjoining the theatre.

'I got Mr d'Arc on his mobile phone,' said Sister Garrett, breathless with relief. 'He's on the M5, and he's going to turn round at the next junction. He says can Sister Curtis get the theatre ready, and Dr McGuire will have to anaesthetise his wife. And, above all, somebody must keep the cord inside her—is Sister Barr around?'

Louise Barr donned surgical gloves and attended to this all-important task, while Sister Garrett removed Anne's clothes and dressed her in a theatre gown and cap. She helped her to sign the consent form, and prepared a warm cot with a separate oxygen cylinder for the baby.

Doreen Nixon was summoned by telephone, and Jill came over from the women's ward to assist Conor, who made his preparations with trembling hands and muttered prayers to every saint in the calendar.

He commenced an intravenous infusion of glucose and saline while Jenny set about preparing her instrument trolley with her usual dexterity. She was conscious of a strange inward calm as she worked and waited for the arrival of the man whose skill and expertise could save this precious baby from death or brain damage.

'Is the cord still pulsating, Louise?' she muttered.

'Yes, about a hundred beats a minute, but getting a bit irregular,' came the low reply.

The news had spread rapidly, and all over the little hospital staff and patients held Sister McGuire and her child in their thoughts at this time of crisis. They all waited for Mr d'Arc.

And there he was, breathless after running from the

car and having hastily put on theatre blues. Doreen assisted him into a sterile gown, and he put on his gloves as the patient was wheeled in, with Louise still protecting the cord. Jenny hastily arranged the sterile towels, and a white-faced Conor stood at his wife's head, administering the anaesthetic—the sleep of life. Louise at last withdrew her hand.

Findlay nodded to Jenny. 'Ready, Sister?'

She nodded and handed him the knife, with a new blade inserted, to make the skin incision, and within ninety seconds from the commencement Findlay lifted out a living male baby which he handed to Sister Garrett.

She placed him in the cot where his little body responded to the stimulus of air. He shuddered, gasped and uttered a thin cry, and as the midwife cleared his mouth and nose he gave another louder cry, a sound which said, 'Here I am, a new arrival in this world!'

In that highly charged atmosphere no one dared give way to emotion. A deep, collective sigh went up from all present, an exhalation of breath after the pent-up tension, but the hearts of all the hearers thrilled to the sound of the baby's cry.

McGuire closed his eyes momentarily and murmured behind his surgical mask. Jenny could not relax her concentration for a moment because she had to act as assistant surgeon to Findlay, clamping blood vessels and aspirating the pelvic cavity after he had removed the placenta. An unusually long umbilical cord hung down from it.

'There's the cause of the trouble,' muttered the surgeon. 'A loop of it must have been lying below the baby for some time, and that would account for the non-engagement of the head. Then as soon as the membranes broke down it came—one of those totally unforeseen emergencies that shake us all out of our complacency.'

The suturing together of the uterine wall, the severed muscle layers and finally the skin took another twenty minutes. Sister Garrett showed the baby to his father, and then took him away to the little nursery to be weighed, labelled and dressed in a vest and nappy.

And it was over. Masks, gowns and gloves were discarded, and Conor gave Anne a pain-relieving injection to take effect when she surfaced to consciousness. He let a stream of pure oxygen flow into her lungs, and then discontinued the intubation.

'Anne,' he murmured brokenly. 'Anne, my heart, can ye hear me? We have a little boy, darlin'…'

All of a sudden Jenny noticed that Findlay was standing motionless, a look of awed wonder on his face as he witnessed the husband's tender care for the wife who had given him a son. She remembered how Findlay had remained faithful to the mistress who had put her career before marriage and the children he would have loved, and on an impulse she gently touched his shoulder.

'Let's leave them alone, Mr d'Arc, just for a minute or two. It seems as if we're intruding.'

Without a word he turned and followed her out of the theatre and into the office that served as a male changing-room, closing the door behind them.

'Jenny. Oh, Jenny, thank God that we were both there, and in time.'

It was then that reaction swept over her. Tears sprung to her eyes, and she swayed slightly.

'Findlay…'

She was caught in his arms and held against him, not gently now but fiercely, almost roughly, as if he were having to overcome resistance, although Jenny offered none. On the contrary, she exalted in his overpowering embrace, the pressure of his lips upon hers, hard and bruising, taking away her speech, her very breath. Willingly she responded, throwing her arms around his neck and burying her fingers in the dark, crisply curling hair.

She heard his heart thudding against hers through the thin blue cotton material and she felt his thighs in close contact with hers, sending a spreading warmth to every part of her body.

And she knew that he desired her—the heat of his passion thrilled like an electric current between them, causing an immediate response in her own body. As his hands pressed against her back and slid down to cover her firm little backside, the sensation was unbelievable, more thrilling than anything she had ever known, and as irresistible.

At last he released her mouth and she gasped for joy, eager to correct any wrong impression he might have had about Steve.

'Findlay, you were mistaken about Dr Forrest,' she panted. 'I'm not—I mean, we're not—I've finished with him.'

'Jenny, my love, it doesn't matter at all. Don't talk about it,' he told her breathlessly, between kisses. 'You're so sweet, Jenny—oh, my dear.'

She clung to him as if for her life. She would have allowed him anything he wanted.

'Jenny, you're the dearest girl in the world.'

She sighed with incredulous delight at hearing these words. They were meant for *her*, Jenny Curtis, here and now—not for another woman at another time. She could have wept for joy.

The sound of rattling bowls and instruments penetrated through to them as Doreen and Jill cleared the theatre and was a reminder of their work, the duty that called them back from this moment of glorious madness. With a half-stifled groan he drew back from her and kissed the top of her ruffled dark head.

'Come, little Jenny, we must go and rejoice with Conor and Anne now,' he said with an effort, taking her hand.

And a great rejoicing it was, all over the hospital, while in Stretbury the happy news was passed on: the McGuires had a little boy, Bernard, named after the brother that Conor had lost.

And nobody rejoiced more than Sister Jenny Curtis, now free to dream that one day Findlay d'Arc would choose her to be his wife...and mother of his children.

True, there could never be another Gabriella, but Jenny was ready and willing to respect her memory. She would be more than content to be the second wife of the man who had so amazingly claimed first place in her own.

She went home to Grannie and Grampy that evening with her heart singing and her feet walking in the clouds, and when the anxious old couple heard the full story of why she was so late they exchanged nods and agreed that the delay had been unavoidable.

'As long as you were with that nice Dr Findlay, dear, we know we needn't worry about you,' smiled Grannie.

CHAPTER EIGHT

ANNE McGUIRE was dozing in a corner bed when Jenny's head popped through the curtains drawn round her. She opened her eyes at once.

'Jenny! Oh, Jenny, I've been thinking about you,' she whispered. 'Conor and I can never repay you for—'

'Shh, Anne, or you'll get me chucked out,' warned Jenny, putting her fingers to her lips. 'Sister Garrett said I was only to take a peep and not utter a word.'

She tiptoed to Anne's side. 'You look pretty good for the morning after. Is young Bernard in the nursery?'

'Yes, he kept crying and Sister Garrett said she'd give him a drink,' sighed Anne. 'I wanted to feed him myself, but she said I could try later.'

She moved her head on the pillows and winced. The intravenous drip was still in place, as well as continuous bladder drainage.

'It'll be easier when I get rid of these attachments!'

Crumbs, thought Jenny, this girl's had major abdominal surgery, yet still wants to breast-feed her baby. What courage women have got!

'I'm just so thrilled for you and Conor, Anne,' she said quietly, putting the little gift she had brought on the bedside-table with a birth congratulations card. 'I'd better go now, and take a peep at Bernard McGuire.'

'Yes, because he owes his life to you, Jenny. Conor was in such a state, I had to take charge and tell him exactly what to do,' Anne told her in a sudden rush of words. 'I was never so thankful to see anybody in my life as I was to see you last night. You and Mr d'Arc saved our baby...'

Her voice quivered and her eyes filled with tears.

'Shh, Anne, not another word. It's all over now,' soothed Jenny, leaning over to kiss the hot cheek. 'Just think about that lovely son of yours and be happy, there's a good girl.'

Returning to the men's ward, she found herself the heroine of the hour. Everybody was talking about the emergency Caesarean section on Sister McGuire, as Anne was still known, and her visitors also called on Sister Curtis.

Lady Hylton's delighted commendations echoed all round the ward, Dr Sellars came to add his congratulations, and Conor McGuire seized Anne in a bear-hug, praising her to the skies in front of her admiring patients and staff.

Later an enormous bouquet arrived with a card from the McGuires, and Anne's mother wept her gratitude. Mrs Crawford was a widow who had remarried and Bernard was her third grandchild, as she explained to Jenny at some length.

In the end Jenny had to insist that she be allowed to attend to her post-ops.

'I must change Mr Smith's dressing,' she told Staff Nurse Barnett. 'If anybody else calls tell them I'm busy!'

She had no sooner removed the dressing when Mavis Barnett, all smiles, came to say that she was required in the office. Jenny rolled her eyes and sighed heavily.

'Not another one! Tell them to hang around while I finish here, will you? Can't leave Mr Smith with his trousers down,' she added with a wink at the elderly patient.

'Please take your time, Sister. I'm happy to wait,' said a voice on the other side of the screen, and Jenny's knees suddenly went weak.

'Er—yes, all right, I'll be with you in two ticks, Mr d'Arc,' she replied.

'May I put the kettle on?' the consultant asked politely.

'I already have, sir,' interposed Mavis Barnett. '*And* set a tray in the office.'

Jenny exchanged a smile with Mr Smith. 'You'll have a cuppa as well when I've taken these alternate clips out! It's healing up beautifully.'

Thank heaven for the patients, she thought gratefully, to keep my feet on the ground and give me time to calm down.

Findlay had poured out two cups of coffee when she joined him in the office. She was determined to be cool and matter-of-fact.

'Good morning, Jenny.' His smile played havoc with her calm common sense. 'I've just been to see our maternity patient.'

Jenny nodded. 'Yes, she's looking good, isn't she, after all the trauma of yesterday?'

He kept his eyes fixed on her. 'And how are *you* feeling today, Jenny?'

'Me? Oh, fine. Conor's been in—he's over the moon about being a daddy. Have you seen him?'

'Jenny, could you possibly arrange to be free next weekend?' he asked abruptly.

'What? Oh, er—well, yes, I'm off then, actually,' she

said shakily, hardly daring to think why he should ask. 'It's the first weekend in July, isn't it?'

'Good! I'm able to take a couple of days off, and I wondered if you'd like to come to Lyme Regis again, Jenny. We enjoyed ourselves so much last time, didn't we?'

Jenny's head whirled. 'Yes, but I—well, yes, that sounds wonderful,' she floundered, unable to take in what she was hearing. 'I'll get in touch with Dennis and Sheila, shall I?'

'Actually, Jenny, I'd like you to be my guest at my parents' home,' he went on. 'My father has asked about you several times, and says he'd love to meet you again.'

Jenny's heart gave such a thump that she clutched the edge of the desk. 'Stay with your *parents*?' she repeated incredulously. 'Have you asked them? I mean, has your mother agreed? She—she didn't exactly take to me, Findlay.'

He smiled and took her hand in his. 'Jenny, I want you to stay with us, and my mother would, of course, welcome any guest of mine. In any case, we'd be out for much of the time. Oh, come on, Jenny, all you have to say is yes!'

While she hesitated he went on quickly, 'The fact is that I'm supposed to be at a conference in Edinburgh the following week, and I probably won't be able to take time off again until around mid-August. And I'd really appreciate spending some time with you before I go away, Jenny,' he added with a look that made her spine tingle.

Does he seriously think I might refuse? she wondered.

'Yes, Findlay, yes, of course, I'd just love to spend a weekend at Lyme with you!'

Her radiant acceptance was followed by a blush in case she sounded over-eager, but when Findlay laughed and gave her a quick kiss on her cheek she gave up trying to be correct. Mavis Barnett remarked to the auxiliary about the stars in Sister Curtis's eyes when she came out of the office.

Throughout the week that followed Jenny seemed to be walking three feet above the ground, and on Tuesday morning the theatre team were aware of a heightened atmosphere and the bright glances exchanged between the consultant and the theatre sister above their surgical masks. There was laughter too over Conor McGuire's comments on fatherhood and his pride in his wife's success at breast-feeding. Findlay had brought Diana Rowland with him as the assistant surgeon, to Jenny's relief.

Back in the ward office she had to submit to Heather Hulland's comments.

'Hey, you're a sly one, Sister Jenny, letting me babble on about Dreamboat d'Arc when all the time you had your own plans for him,' teased the Australian girl. 'And how do you propose to tackle the problems you warned *me* about? The ghost of wifey number one and the ma-in-law from—'

'Oh, Heather, please, *please* don't ever tell anyone I said that!' implored Jenny. 'I was only trying to persuade myself that—I mean, I thought that he thought that I was having an affair with—er—somebody else.'

'It all sounds too complicated for me but don't worry, sweetie, I'd say you've got him eating out of your lily-white hand.'

'Thanks, Heather. Let's hope I can win over his

mother, too,' answered Jenny, who was by no means sure that she could.

As the days went by Jenny's mixed feelings about staying with the d'Arcs was overtaken by another worry, something she did her best to ignore but which would not go away.

By Thursday she had to face the fact that she was in almost constant abdominal pain and feeling increasingly unwell. Still she refused to give way to the warning signs, for she felt that nothing must be allowed to spoil this weekend on which her very future might depend. For Jenny now believed that Findlay was seriously considering her as a second wife, and that this visit was a kind of test at which she might succeed or fail.

Her grandparents were delighted to hear of the invitation, and everything seemed set for the fulfilment of Jenny's dearest dreams—except for this horrid sub-acute appendicitis which was threatening to ruin everything.

Well, she wouldn't let it. She gritted her teeth and absolutely refused to give way until after the weekend when she would go to see Dr Sellars. Definitely.

Findlay said he would call for her at around six-thirty at Bailey's Cottage on Friday evening, and Heather insisted that she left the ward at three-thirty.

'You've put in plenty of overtime lately, Jenny, so off you go—I'll hold the fort for the next coupla days while you live it up with Dreamboat. Take care now, sweetie, and don't let the old lady spoil the fun!'

After Jenny had gone Heather confided to the other staff nurse that she didn't like the look of Jenny at all.

'Y'know, Mave, I have this hunch that our girlie's trying to hide something. And if she is he'll find it out.'

Right up until the moment Findlay rang the doorbell,

Jenny had lain on her bed, hoping against hope that this latest flare-up of inflammation would subside as it had done on previous occasions. An agonising and embarrassing bout of diarrhoea had left her feeling weak and shaky. Her mouth was dry and her tongue furred. She had a moment's panic, then summoned up all her resolution.

'Listen, you're going to be all right and not utter a word,' she snarled at her reflection in the old triple mirror. It stared back at her with flushed cheeks and overbright eyes that looked unconvinced.

Findlay greeted her with a light kiss, his hands briefly touching her shoulders. He also kissed Grannie and chatted with Grampy for a few minutes.

'I hope you don't take out the screw-top jar in company, Will!' he grinned.

'Course I don't, Doctor,' replied the old man, quite shocked at the suggestion. 'I only use it when I'm down the garden!'

The old couple followed them out to the car, smiling and clearly happy with their granddaughter's companion. They waved until the car was out of sight and heading for the M5 motorway.

'Now, Jenny, tell me everything you've been doing this week,' said Findlay pleasantly, wanting to put her at ease. 'Whether at work or at home, anything's that's interested you—fire away!'

And it was at that very moment that Jenny was seized with the worst pain she had ever known: it was like a knife sinking into her stomach, taking her breath away. She doubled up involuntarily, pulling on her seat belt. With a sharp cry she straightened up and clenched her hands in agony.

'Jenny, what is it, what's the matter, for God's sake?' cried Findlay, swerving the car as he briefly took his left hand off the steering-wheel. He had been just about to take the slip-road onto the motorway but pulled back and turned onto the grass verge at the side of it, where he stopped the car and gave his attention to the girl writhing beside him. He felt for her pulse, noted her deathly white face and rapid, shallow breathing. She was clutching the lower part of her tummy.

'Pain, Findlay—such a *pain*,' she gasped, her brown eyes imploring his help.

Findlay gave her one more horrified look, and went into action.

'Hold on, Jenny, keep still and don't panic,' he muttered as he turned the car back onto the road they had left and headed for Stretbury Memorial Hospital, driving as urgently as Conor McGuire had driven his wife just eight days ago. Into the drive and up to the front entrance they sped, and Jenny heard him shout for a stretcher trolley.

Hands took hold of her and she heard herself moan as she was lifted out of the car and wheeled towards the women's ward. Then Sister Barr was taking off her clothes, a thermometer was thrust into her mouth and she felt a constriction around her left arm as her blood pressure was recorded. All around her voices spoke, muttered, shouted—and the pain went on stabbing into her flesh.

Findlay towered above her, his long fingers feeling her naked tummy—palpating, pressing gently. She groaned out loud, and Louise held her hand.

'Give five milligrams of diamorphine stat, and bring me an intravenous giving-set,' he rapped out, the curtness of his voice not quite concealing his fear. 'Is there anybody in this place who can assist me with a laparotomy and prepare the theatre?'

Somebody said, 'Sister Absalom.'

'Thank God. Have her called. And McGuire.'

Jenny felt a prick in her arm, and then he was talking to her alone.

'Right, Jenny, now I want the truth. Answer me honestly and I'll do my best for you. What was the date of your last period?'

Jenny's thoughts were disconnected because of the pain.

'About—er—the beginning—the first week in June, I think,' she mumbled vaguely, wondering what such a question had to do with her present agony. She moaned involuntarily again and he leaned over her, his piercing gaze searching her face.

'Don't play about, Jenny, and don't lie to me—just help me to help you. When did you last have intercourse with Dr Forrest?'

Even as the red-hot needles of pain thrust into her belly Jenny wilted with shame and distress at hearing these words, so cold and unsympathetic. Tears gathered in her eyes.

'Never, not—ever,' she wailed feebly, staring back into those two ice-blue eyes probing hers.

'I'm going to have to find out, Jenny, so please don't waste time denying what we both know,' he said curtly. 'You had a relationship with Forrest and, all right, I know it's over now, and I never intended to mention it—but now we have to face facts. You're pregnant, aren't you? And this is an ectopic, a tubal rupture, right? I'm going to have to operate, and you'll lose the

Fallopian tube on the affected side—you realise that, don't you?'

Jenny made a superhuman effort to answer him, speaking through rigidly clenched teeth.

'Is—is not possible,' she gasped. 'Please—believe—'

But he had turned away from her without another word. The pain began to ease a little as the diamorphine injection took effect, but a sensation of utter desolation took its place as footsteps came and went, telephones rang, doors opened and closed, light turned to darkness and back again. Disembodied voices reached her from various directions.

'The blood's gone off to be cross-matched, and meanwhile we've got two litres of plasma.'

'Dr Rowland's on her way over to assist, Mr d'Arc.'

'Will you sign this consent form, Jenny?' This was Louise Barr. 'I'll help you to put a cross just here, see, beside my finger—that's right. No capped teeth? No jewellery? I've got your watch and the little silver cross on a chain.'

'Hi, sweetie, just hang in there, and I'll come and see you afterwards, OK?'

'Has somebody got in touch with her relatives?'

'There's only those old grandparents as far as I know.'

'Is there a mother somewhere?'

'She'll need to go in as soon as Theatre's set up.'

'Sister Absalom says she's ready when you are, Mr d'Arc.'

And then Conor's voice speaking gently, close to her ear.

'Hallo, Jenny darlin'. Feelin' sleepy? Good. You know we'll all take very good care o' ye. Now, you'll feel a little prick on the back o' yer hand…steady now…'

A terrible sense of loneliness swept over Jenny during those last few seconds before the intravenous Pentothal wafted her into oblivion, but just before that happened she saw those two blue eyes again, regarding her over the top of a surgical mask.

And heard his voice speaking to her.

'I'm here, Jenny. You can trust me to look after you.'

She gave a long sigh and closed her eyes as the lights went out and all sounds faded into absolute nothingness.

It was like rising to the surface of a heaving sea, up out of the dark waters of the subconscious to a bewildering jumble of sensations—a sore tummy, a parched mouth and two female voices floating in the air somewhere above her head.

'She's coming round. Hello, Jenny!' said one of them.

'It's over now, dear. You've had an operation and everything's all right now.' Jenny recognised Sister Absalom's warm West Indian accent.

'Water,' she managed to croak in a dry-as-dust, gravelly voice, quite unlike her own. 'Water…please.'

She was lifted up on a bed and pillows were put behind her while a glass was held to her lips. Cold water had never tasted so good, but it was taken away too soon. She licked dry lips and drifted back into sleep. When she woke again somebody was wiping her face with a wet flannel. It had to be late because night Sister Pilgrim was at her side with a syringe and needle. And she seemed to be talking to somebody.

'Yes, she's stable, sir. Pulse and blood pressure within reasonable limits, temperature thirty-nine point five. I'm just giving the intravenous cephalosporin. She's due for the Flagyl at midnight.'

Then there was a man's voice, sounding strained.

'Thank heaven. What about the abdominal drain?'

'Blood-stained fluid only, sir, not very much.'

There was a pause and what sounded like a deep sigh, then Sister Pilgrim spoke again.

'Her grandparents telephoned again, and I said they could visit tomorrow.'

'Poor old souls. I've tried to reassure them as much as I can. Oh, my God...'

'Would you like a cup of tea, sir? You look all in.'

Was that a tall shadow of a man standing at the foot of the bed? Jenny was not sure whether he was Findlay or a dream. She closed her eyes and when she opened them again he was gone. There was only a man seated on a chair beside the bed, his dark head held between his hands as the very first light of dawn began to filter through the curtains.

Jenny remembered very little about that weekend, and passed the hours in a drug-induced haze, out of which faces, hands and voices came and went. When she saw Grannie weeping she wanted to cry too, but Grampy said they mustn't upset her.

'I know, Will, but it's seeing her with all these tubes and bottles,' sobbed Grannie. Will Curtis patted her shoulder.

'Now, Doris, just stop that piping and be thankful that Dr Findlay was there to take her appendix out!' He then wiped his own eyes with a large handkerchief, and their place was taken by Dr Sellars who looked grave when he came and stood beside her with Sister Absalom.

'Gangrenous appendix with free pus in the peritoneal

cavity—a few more hours and there'd have been gener-
alised peritonitis and septicaemia,' whispered a man's
voice. 'I removed the appendix and did a peritoneal
lavage, leaving an abdominal drain. She's on maximum
dosage antibiotics intravenously for forty-eight hours,
then possibly oral—just have to wait and see.'

'Good heavens, d'Arc, how on earth did she manage
to keep going? And *why*?' asked Sellars's voice in bewilderment.

There was no reply, and Jenny felt curiously detached.
Nurses came to record observations, empty the drainage
bags, change the saline and dextrose drip and write the
fluid intake and output on one of several charts at the
foot of the bed.

And there was another presence, never far away—
standing or sitting beside her, offering sips of iced water,
wiping her face, sometimes holding her hand and saying
her name.

'Jenny.'

'Findlay?' she asked huskily.

He came to her side at once. 'Yes, I'm here, my love.
Is there anything you want, anything I can do for you?
Something I can get for you?'

Jenny tried to think, but all that came into her head
was the thought of how awful she must look with her
tangled hair and dry skin. Her eyes turned slowly towards the toilet-bag hanging by her bedside locker. He
followed her look, and with a flash of realisation he unhooked the bag and opened it. He took out a comb, and
also found a jar of moisturising cream.

'Shall I try my skill at hairdressing, Jenny?'

It was a most unusual sensation as he ran the comb
through her dark mop. She felt him re-parting it and

carefully smoothing it down into the neat, cap-like style she had worn to the midsummer party. The touch of his sensitive surgeon's fingers separating the strands and tugging gently at a tangle above her left ear was extraordinarily pleasing.

'There, is that better?' he asked, adding a finishing touch with the comb. Jenny smiled.

'Shall I cream your face now?'

She nodded and lay back on her pillows. A delicious contentment engulfed her as he dipped his fingertips in the jar and smoothed the light, fresh-smelling cream over her forehead, cheeks, nose and chin. Like an expert beautician, he feathered it carefully around her eyes and mouth, using tiny upward strokes. Finally he took a tissue from a box on her locker and wiped off the surplus, leaving her skin cool and moist.

'Thank you,' she managed to say, feeling distinctly more human.

'You're so sweet, Jenny.'

There were many things that each of them wanted to say to the other, but now was not the time. Jenny was not well enough, and Findlay was all too aware of her weakness. Yet something had been conveyed without words as he attended to her appearance, so essential to a woman's well-being.

He spent the whole of that weekend with her, the time they should have shared at Lyme, and by Sunday evening Jenny had begun to improve noticeably. Her mind cleared and she began to make sense of her surroundings.

'Sorry about our lost weekend, Findlay,' she murmured with a wry smile.

'Dear Jenny, I'm sorry about a whole lot of things,'

he replied sombrely, wondering how much she remembered of that terrible exchange before she went under the anaesthetic and not wanting to distress her by recalling it.

There was a long pause and, as if she partly understood his thoughts, she finally replied quietly.

'You saved my life, Findlay, and that's all that matters now.'

Sitting beside the bed, he picked up her hand which was lying on the sheet, kissed it reverently and held it to his face. Jenny closed her eyes and wondered if by any chance she had died and landed up in heaven...

After a long interval she spoke again. 'You'll be due back at Bristol tomorrow, won't you?'

'Yes, Jenny, I shall be leaving tonight, knowing that you're going to be all right. I'll come and see you again, of course.'

'Didn't you say something about a meeting you had to attend soon in Scotland?' she asked.

'Yes, in Edinburgh. I was prepared to cancel it after your operation, Jenny, and I still might.'

'What do you mean, cancel it?' she asked in astonishment, turning towards him. 'There's no reason to miss it on my account. I'm feeling so much better—of course you must go, Findlay!'

'I shall see.' His fingers tightened round her hand. 'Where will you go when you're discharged, Jenny? Neither Sellars nor I are happy about you going to your grandparents.'

'Oh, let's cross that bridge when we come to it,' she smiled, though thrilled to know that he would have cancelled his engagement in Edinburgh for her sake.

*   *   *

By Monday morning she was making rapid progress—
skilful surgery and powerful antibiotics were taking their
effect, combined with Jenny's natural resilience and
positive attitude. Other visitors began to arrive. Anne
McGuire and baby Bernard; her grandparents, of course,
who came each afternoon; Peter and Brenda Gould who
had heard that she was ill and came to wish her a speedy
recovery, and a whole avalanche of cards, flowers and
gifts poured in.

'You'll be able to open a shop with all those bottles
of fruit squash, sweetie,' quipped Heather when she
dropped in from the men's ward.

Lady Margaret Hylton was horrified at hearing of the
grave emergency and the operation findings. She was
equally shocked when she realised that the newly ap-
pointed sister had carried on working in pain and discomfort from an untreated and potentially dangerous
condition. She immediately silenced Jenny's regrets at
going off sick during a staff crisis.

'My dear Sister Curtis, how could you so neglect
yourself?' she asked reproachfully. 'When I think what
might have happened— How do you think I would have
felt if—?'

She shook her head and pointed out that the staff
situation had been greatly eased by the arrival of Sister
Absalom and Staff Nurse Hulland. Jenny must not dream
of returning to duty until she was completely fit, she
insisted.

'Not that Mr d'Arc will allow you to do so, my dear,'
she added with a rather significant look. 'He has been
most dreadfully upset about you.'

On Wednesday Dennis and Sheila drove up from
Somerset, bringing not only their good wishes but a firm

invitation to spend her convalescence at Dewsfold.

'Mum and Dad couldn't possibly look after you, Jen, and you wouldn't get a proper rest at all,' said Dennis. 'As soon as you get your discharge date give me a ring and I'll come to fetch you. You've done a great job with Dad, and now it's our turn. No arguments, it's all settled—OK?'

Jenny was touched by their willing hospitality, and saw no reason to decline such a kind offer. It was also good news for Findlay when he visited her on Thursday evening.

'Now I know that you're going to be well looked after, Jenny, I feel better about going to the conference tomorrow,' he told her. 'I've been asked to give some lectures afterwards so I could be away for ten days or so, possibly longer. Let me know when you go to Dewsfold so that I can keep in touch.'

His eyes lingered on her face. 'Somehow or other I've got to say goodbye to you, Jenny. It's a little easier now that you're looking so much better, but you can have no idea how much I   '

He broke off and bit his lip.

'You must send me a postcard, Findlay!' she said brightly, though suddenly feeling perilously close to tears.

His kiss on her lips was as light as the touch of a butterfly's wing, and she felt his hand briefly rest upon her shoulder. And then he was gone, and for a few moments she lay back on her pillows and let the tears flow.

Until she noticed the package on her locker, gift-wrapped and inviting. She reached out for it eagerly, undoing the paper and giving a gasp of surprised delight when an elegant pale leather vanity case was revealed.

Inside it she found a collection of top-quality skin-care products with matching shampoo and hair conditioner. Two famous and wildly expensive perfumes were included, and a hand-written note that simply said, 'For Jenny'. It was the most luxurious gift she had ever received, but especially precious because it was from Findlay d'Arc.

For a long while she sat holding it open before her, revelling in the delicious fragrances and dreaming of the man who had chosen them just for her.

CHAPTER NINE

'YOU'RE looking quite tanned already, Jenny. I can't believe it's only three weeks since your op,' said Sheila as they lounged on garden chairs in the sunshine.

'Nineteen days, to be precise,' answered the invalid, reaching for another scone. 'Honestly, I feel such an awful fraud, especially when I think of my poor post-ops on the men's ward.'

Jenny found that she was enjoying being part of a family, sharing in the day-to-day events of their lives. She was feeling better than for many months past now that the offending appendix had been removed.

'So, when can we look forward to seeing Dr Gorgeous again?' asked Sheila pointedly.

'This weekend, probably. He says he hopes to spend a couple of days at Lyme after Edinburgh,' replied Jenny. 'Visiting his parents,' she added

'And *you*! I've seen your post, remember, and I don't think he's missed a day.'

Jenny smiled a little uncertainly. She was not sure how she felt about her next meeting with Findlay. The close intimacy of her immediate post-operative phase was hazy and unreal in her memory. In fact, she was not quite sure how much of it was true and how much imagined. The beautiful vanity case was real enough, and had definitely impressed Sheila.

'Wow, Jenny, he *must* be serious!' she had exclaimed when helping Jenny to unpack her belongings. 'How

159

imaginative of him, to know the importance of a woman's appearance!' Jenny had closed her eyes and remembered the touch of his fingers on her hair and face as she'd lain in her hospital bed.

A series of postcards had arrived from Edinburgh, and a letter in which he wrote that he would be leaving on Thursday morning. Today was Wednesday so Jenny was totally unprepared for Sheila's next words.

'Why, Mr d'Arc! Findlay! What a surprise! Jenny wasn't expecting you before the weekend!'

Jenny sat bolt upright on the lounger and turned her head to face their visitor.

'My dear Jenny—and Sheila—hello! I tried the door and got no answer so I came round to the back. Jenny, you're looking wonderful.'

He towered above her for a moment, then lowered his long frame onto the grass, drawing up his knees to sit beside her.

'We—we were just talking about you,' she stammered, holding out her hand which he took and held.

'I'll go and make some more tea,' said Sheila, tactfully getting up and putting their cups on the tray. 'Have you eaten lately, Findlay?'

'Don't bother about me. I'm fine, thanks, Sheila,' he said. 'Actually, I'm hoping to persuade this young lady to come out with me for a drive.'

Sheila smiled and nodded as she went indoors.

'This is such a surprise, Findlay,' murmured Jenny in happy confusion. 'When did you leave Edinburgh?'

'At first light this morning. It was no good, I couldn't wait any longer so I cancelled my final lecture and got in the car. And here I am, my Jenny, the happiest man in the world!'

Carefully, gently, he put his arms around her and kissed her cheek. 'Oh, it's good, good, good to be with you again.'

'You too—I mean, me too, Findlay.' He had lost none of his power to drive every coherent thought out of her head. Every nerve ending thrilled at his closeness.

'Tell me, Jenny, how do you feel now? I mean, really?'

'Just fine, honestly. I've been thoroughly spoiled and shockingly lazy! And, to be truthful, just the tiniest bit bored now. Perhaps when Amanda and William break up from school I'll have more to occupy my time. But, Findlay, how are you?'

He ran his hand down her cheek, never once taking his eyes from her. 'All right now. My head and my heart have been in two different places, Jenny!'

She thought how much younger he seemed, even boyish as he grinned at her. 'So come on, Sister Curtis, come out with me—now!'

'But you've been driving all day, all that distance—'

'My car had wings.'

'Oh, Findlay!' She giggled, but then a sudden thought struck her.

'You don't mean to take me to your home, do you?'

'No—I mean somewhere we can talk. Alone, just the two of us.'

'Sounds all right to me,' she said, relieved. 'Lead the way, Mr d'Arc!'

'Mind you behave yourselves,' laughed Sheila as he gave Jenny his arm and walked her to the car, settling her into the passenger seat and fastening her safety belt.

'There's a nice old teashop in Lyme where we can chat at our leisure,' he told her. 'I've got lots to say to you—if you're well enough to hear it, Jenny. Are you?' he asked, giving her a sideways look as he drove.

'Of course I am.' She tried to sound matter-of-fact, though her thoughts raced on in anticipation of what he had to say.

Seated in a cosy alcove with a tray of tea and currant buns, he hesitated at first.

'Where to begin, Jenny? I think perhaps I should go back to that morning in April when I first saw you. Do you remember how I followed you to the Hylton annexe when the list was finished?'

'Of course I do, Findlay. But could you go back further than that?' she asked quietly. 'Try beginning with how you felt after you lost Gabriella.'

He looked at her sharply. 'Do you really want to hear about that time in my life? I was at a very loose end then, just drifting. I was approaching forty, and I'd had a good life—a growing practice in Paris, a fair amount of travel, especially to Rome where I mixed with the social set that always surrounded Gabriella. You could say that we burned the candle at both ends, but it was, well, a young man's life.

'Then within less than six months it was all over, not only my life with Gabriella, but everything—the social scene, the Paris practice. I turned my back on it all—our former friends, everybody. I knew that it was finished, though I had no idea what to do or where to go.'

He paused to see her reaction. She was watching him intently, with tender compassion in her soft brown eyes. 'Go on.'

'Then I met up with a friend from training days who'd been working in South America, and he showed me these slides he'd taken of the place—a mission station with a small hospital and a mobile clinic that went out to remote villages. It sounded as if it might be the opportunity I was looking for, a chance to disappear.

'So I wrote, and was offered this job straight away—two years of hard work in fairly primitive conditions, as I've told you. A good life, Jenny, and I don't regret a single day of it. Only...' He paused again.

'Only—you developed infective hepatitis and had to leave?' she prompted gently.

'Yes, Jenny, I did—and it seemed as if the time was right. Two years away from the world, working alongside a dedicated mission team had taught me a lot of things about myself, and I was beginning to feel that I should return to the challenge of a consultancy, as well as keeping a weather eye on my parents. So when I saw this Bristol vacancy advertised—'

He stopped speaking, and looked full into her eyes.

'At the time I hadn't the remotest idea about remarriage or any kind of relationship. But that was before I met you.'

Jenny hid her turmoil beneath an assumed calmness as the direction of his words became clear.

'Perhaps not consciously at first, but as I got to know you I knew you were what I really needed, Jenny—someone to love and to share my life. I never thought it would happen again after Gabriella, but I learned that fate has a way of surprising us.'

Jenny could only go on gazing at him across the table, unable to trust herself to speak.

'And then, no sooner had I admitted to myself that I was in love with you than Forrest came up with his prior claim. Oh, Jenny, what jealousy I felt towards that man! He always seemed to be gloating over his—well, his association with you. Yet somehow I couldn't give up hoping.' His face broke into a reminiscent grin. 'And when we spent that afternoon with the children at Lyme I made up my mind to steal you away from Forrest if I possibly could!'

Jenny stared. The teacakes lay untasted on the plate.

'But, Findlay, several people thought—in fact, I wondered myself—that you and Diana Rowland were—'

'Ah, dear Diana. Yes, I must confess that I confided in her, Jenny. She had noticed with a woman's intuition how I felt about you, and she actually encouraged me to press ahead! She didn't think you cared that much for Forrest. But then at that midsummer party when I saw you both in the medical quarters—'

'Stop, Findlay, stop, don't mention that!' she interrupted. 'It wasn't how it looked, and if you'd only stayed and not dashed off as you did—'

'Jenny, I didn't trust myself. I was afraid I'd thrash the man. Believe me, I could have killed him.'

'So could I,' muttered Jenny. 'You should have stayed to watch.'

'How I managed to work with him after that I do not know—it was terrible. Yet I was as furious with myself as with him.' He gave a short, self-deprecating laugh.

'And then came the scare over Anne McGuire,' recalled Jenny, 'and that emergency Caesarean section!'

'Yes, that was it. I couldn't hold back any longer,' he admitted grimly. 'And when I kissed you you responded to me, and that was when I decided that the fight was still on and I was in with rather more than a fighting chance. And so I asked you to spend a weekend in Lyme Regis.'

'And instead you ended up removing my appendix.'

She grinned ruefully. 'And *you* thought that I was having a—'

'Jenny, don't say it! Just don't *say* it. Don't remind me of how I behaved. I was beside myself, and couldn't think straight. And when I discovered the state of your appendix and the— Oh, my God, the agony you must have been through, the fact that I was only just in time to prevent— Oh, Jenny, Jenny! I'll never forget that night as long as I live. Never.'

She put out a hand and covered his as it lay on the table. 'But you *were* in time, Findlay, and you saved me. Look at me now.'

He looked and saw the soft glow in her eyes, the deep happiness of a woman who knows that she is loved. He caught his breath, and his voice shook slightly as he continued.

'Sometimes it takes a crisis to get things into focus, Jenny. I'd been a self-centred idiot, but I was forced to read my destiny that night—that bitter night when I sat beside you and prayed. By the time morning came I knew what I had to say to you, but you were much too ill to hear it.'

Jenny dimly remembered the constant presence at her bedside, day and night, over that first critical forty-eight hours.

'So can you say it now, Findlay?' she asked softly. 'I think I'm well enough to hear it, don't you?'

Their fingers intertwined on the table.

'I love you, Jenny Curtis.'

'I know, Findlay d'Arc. And I love you.'

The sounds of the teashop receded as they gazed into each other's eyes, enclosed in a world of their own.

'Then you know what comes next, dearest Jenny. When will you marry me?'

She laughed softly. 'Tomorrow, Findlay, if it was up to me! But there are lots of things to talk about, aren't there?'

'What things? What's more important than marrying you?'

'Well, there's your future career, for a start.'

'I'll renew my contract at Bristol in October.'

'And there's Grannie and Grampy.'

'We'll find a house near enough to keep an eye on them, somewhere between Bristol and Stretbury.'

'And my job—'

'You won't need a job once we're married, not if...' He chuckled mischievously, leaving the rest of the prophecy unsaid.

'And there's the question of your parents, Findlay.' A note of real anxiety now crept into her voice. 'Your mother will be upset, I know she will.'

'My darling Jenny, don't worry about Mother,' he said quickly. 'She's always been a bit possessive, which is why I don't go home too often, but she's always supported me in my career. And now I want to present you to them both as my future wife.'

'No! Oh, please, *no!*' she implored. 'Let's wait a while, Findlay, before we tell other people. I'd rather keep it to ourselves until I'm over my convalescence. And when the time comes you'll have to break it gently to your parents, and not just spring it on them. *Please*, Findlay.'

Her agitation made Findlay reproach himself for burdening her with an emotional situation so soon after her illness, and he was all apologies.

'All right, my love, all right. We'll keep it under wraps for the time being,' he agreed. 'Only you must give *me* a wedding date to look forward to! What about September?'

'Findlay, I think we'll need more time than that. I was thinking of Christmas.'

'*Christmas*? That's much too far away, Jenny. You surely can't expect me to wait that long!'

She laughed at his stricken expression. 'Well, let's split the difference and say the end of October—provisionally, that is.'

'It looks as if I shall have to settle for that, then—provisionally,' he said with a mock groan. 'Only I really would like to take you to see the parents tomorrow, Jenny. Papa was so disappointed when we had to cancel our weekend, and he's enquired about you several times. Don't worry, we won't mention our engagement,' he promised.

Enfolded in her new-found happiness, Jenny felt she could hardly refuse, though the very thought of confronting Fiona d'Arc made her nervous. She told herself that it would be an opportunity to make friends with her future mother-in-law, but she was fairly certain that Findlay underestimated his mother's opposition to the idea of him remarrying. She resolved to do her best, for the sake of the man she loved.

Tea on the terrace of the elegant house, with Fiona d'Arc presiding over a Georgian silver tea-service, was a somewhat constrained affair, although Findlay's high spirits were impossible to hide. Henri exchanged some knowing looks with his son, and sent a few quiet smiles in Jenny's direction, too. She felt certain that Henri d'Arc guessed the situation and it added to her awkwardness, as if they were all conspiring to deceive Mrs d'Arc.

'More tea, Miss Curtis?' asked her hostess with formal politeness.

'Thank you, I'd love another cup. I do wish you'd call me Jenny,' she answered in her friendliest manner. Mrs d'Arc raised her eyebrows slightly but did not take up the invitation, and Jenny felt dashed, unable to think of anything to say.

'How did the Edinburgh conference go, Findlay?' asked his mother.

'Oh, well enough,' he replied easily. 'I got up on my hind legs at the required times and talked about recent advances in gynaecology—the new thinking about post-menopausal hormonal activity, mainly. By contrast, I also lectured about the Third World, pointing out the incredibly primitive conditions women have to endure in under-developed countries. All rather ironic, really,' he added, turning down the corners of his mouth in a deprecating grimace. Jenny was astonished.

'I didn't realise that you covered such a lot of ground, Findlay,' she remarked. 'Were there any delegates from overseas?'

Mrs d'Arc replaced her cup on its saucer with a gesture of superiority.

'My dear Miss Curtis, this was a highly prestigious top-level international symposium, and Findlay was a principal speaker. You clearly have no idea of his position.'

Jenny coloured and looked abashed, remembering that he had been prepared to forego the conference altogether if he had not considered her well enough to leave.

'Oh, come off it, Mother,' said Findlay with a modest

shrug. 'There were plenty of older and more experienced brains there than mine!'

'Indeed, Findlay?' Fiona's voice managed to convey both affection for her son and scorn for the ignorance of others. 'Then I wonder why you have been offered a professorship in Paris, over and above some of these better brains?'

'Which I will *not* be taking up, incidentally, Mother,' he returned quickly. 'My Paris life is in the past. I shall be staying on at Bristol.'

Jenny was astounded. Clearly Findlay was of far greater eminence in his field than she had realised. There were still a lot of things she didn't know about this man who had asked her to marry him and share his future.

Henri attempted to rescue her by asking about her nursing career, but she felt that she had to be careful not to leave his wife out of the conversation.

'We had a letter from Padua last week, Findlay,' Mrs d'Arc said suddenly. 'Signore and Signora Rasi would like us to visit them some time this year. All three of us.'

'That's very kind of them, but I'm afraid I'm pretty well booked up now for the year,' Findlay replied, shaking his head. 'How are they?'

'Well, as you might expect on the anniversary of Gabriella's passing,' his mother said with a hint of reproach. 'Henri and I feel it too, of course, but they are her parents.'

Turning to Jenny, she spoke with cool deliberation.

'It's just three years since Findlay's wife died in Venice. At a hospice on the Lido, actually. We were all there,' she said in a tone that reminded Jenny of her former words—'There can be no other woman for him after Gabriella.'

There was a deathly silence, during which Jenny's indignation rose. She suddenly decided to make a clear statement of her opinion, whether it was well received or not. She drew a deep breath, and looked straight at Findlay's mother.

'Findlay has told me about Gabriella,' she said levelly. 'How beautiful and talented she was—a woman who lived life to the full. I feel quite certain that a woman like Gabriella would not want—would not approve of this sadness, this mourning going on year after year.'

Henri lost no time in agreeing with this sentiment. '*Très bien*! I am sure that Jenny is right, *ma chérie*,' he said firmly, and Findlay also gave her an encouraging smile. Mrs d'Arc's mouth hardened, and she did not reply.

Having shot her bolt, Jenny felt limp and her head ached.

'Will you all excuse me now? I feel rather tired,' she said, looking imploringly at Findlay and unable to keep a tremor out of her voice.

'Of course, darling Jenny. Forgive me, you must be exhausted,' he replied at once, standing up and helping her to her feet. She had gone very pale, and he put his arm around her waist as he led her down from the terrace and settled her in the car. Henri accompanied them, expressing his regret at having tired the young lady and begging her to visit them again.

Jenny lay back in the passenger seat and closed her eyes as Findlay nosed the car out of the drive.

'You mustn't mind Mother, Jenny. She'd be exactly the same with any other girl,' he said soothingly. 'I do apologise on her behalf, though, especially as I'm absolutely certain that she'll accept you as a daughter and learn to love you when she knows that we're going to be married. I honestly think that the sooner we tell her the better it will be.'

Jenny didn't reply because she could not agree. Besides, she felt too tired to argue, and feared she might burst into tears if another word was said about Fiona d'Arc. She felt chilled—a shadow had fallen across her happiness, like a dark cloud obscuring the sun.

After Findlay had returned to Bristol the following day Jenny faced a further three weeks of convalescence at Dewsfold. She felt she needed the time to think about future plans. Findlay had said that Christmas was too far away for their wedding, but Jenny was beginning to think that a six-month engagement might be needed to get everything sorted out, and she didn't only mean practical considerations like where they would live, or even Findlay's future career choices.

She loved him and longed to make him happy. The last thing she wanted was a rift between him and the mother who adored him and was so proud of his achievements. Yet how was she to deal with Fiona's open hostility?

After Amanda and William had broken up for the summer holidays Jenny found that her young cousins took up a lot of her time, leaving less opportunity to brood over the problem that threatened to overshadow her happiness.

Findlay sent her letters and cards, and said he would come to collect her in mid-August to take her back to Bailey's Cottage. She expected to be ready to return to duty at the beginning of September when the new senior nursing administrator would be taking up her post and the staff crisis would be over.

Jenny was anxious to know how her grandparents had coped in her absence, and Findlay reassured her, having been to see them.

'We can only wait and see how they go on, Jenny, and they seem to be all right at present,' he wrote. 'As long as they want to remain in their own home and can manage to look after themselves, with the help of the social services, they should be allowed to do so. If a day comes when they need residential care we know we have the Hylton annexe close at hand.'

Jenny noticed how he said 'we', as if he already shared responsibility for the old couple, yet at the same time her relationship with Fiona d'Arc troubled her all the more. What *was* she to do? She even considered taking the bull by the horns and calling on the d'Arcs unannounced, telling them of the engagement and of her longing to be accepted.

But her courage failed. Suppose Fiona rejected her to her face and accused her of taking advantage of Findlay in a weak moment? Things would then be even worse. Besides, Jenny felt that it should be Findlay who broke the news.

And so the summer days sped by, and the time came for her departure from Dewsfold. Findlay planned to spend a couple of days in Lyme, taking Jenny to the places he had intended to show her on the ill-fated weekend of her collapse.

It was heaven.

'Who wants to see the donkey sanctuary at Sidmouth?' he asked.

'*We* do, Dr Findlay!' cried Amanda and William in unison, leaping into the back seat of his car.

Jenny was deeply impressed by the well-maintained haven for hundreds of donkeys, many of them rescued from lives of neglect and cruelty. Their soft, trusting eyes went straight to her heart, and she forgot everything else as she stroked the harmless creatures who responded so readily to kindness.

'A lot of these chaps work for their keep, giving rides to handicapped children,' said Findlay. 'Look, there are some here today.'

'Oh, can I have a ride on one?' asked William.

Jenny's brown eyes misted over as she watched a little Down's syndrome girl eagerly climbing onto the back of patient Gypsy, who was then led away to a paddock where others were waiting.

'How wonderful,' she breathed softly. 'Oh, isn't there a lesson to be learned from this place? Wouldn't the whole world be changed if only everybody...'

She was at a loss for words to express the spirit of sheer goodness and kindness that pervaded the sanctuary.

'Let's just be glad that these fortunate ones have found a good home,' said Findlay gently. 'And, yes, William, I think we can arrange a ride for you. Let's go to the office and ask for a good-tempered mount!'

When the children had reluctantly left the donkeys Findlay drove to Lyme, saying that he had something to show Jenny and Amanda in the guildhall. In an upstairs room they came upon three ladies who were busily stitching away at an enormous tapestry, showing scenes from British and American history. They said it was called the New World tapestry, and on payment of one

pound anybody could insert one stitch and so become a
patron of this masterpiece. Findlay produced two pound
coins, and Amanda sat down to add one blue wool stitch
to a wide expanse of embroidered sky.

'You should have put it up here, not down there,'
grinned William as his sister pulled the needle up
through the heavy material.

'No, I shouldn't, silly! Anyway, it's Jenny's turn now.
Where will you put yours, Jenny?'

'Oh, I'll have a green stitch and add it to this tree,'
said Jenny, taking the threaded needle.

'Mind you don't prick your finger and fall asleep for
a hundred years,' quipped Findlay, winking at Amanda.

'No problem in your case,' replied one of the embroi-
dresses, smiling at Jenny. 'One kiss from this handsome
prince and you'd soon wake up again!'

Jenny avoided their eyes as she placed her stitch, and
when she rose Findlay put a restraining hand on her
shoulder. When she turned to face him he put his forefinger under her chin and planted a very public kiss on
the tip of her nose, much to the ladies' amusement.

Amanda stared. 'So you *are* going to marry Jenny, Dr
Findlay!' she said with all the superiority of an eleven-
year-old.

'That's right, Amanda, the rumours are true,' he whispered, confidentially tapping the side of his nose. 'Now,
who's for a picnic lunch on the Undercliff?'

By the time they arrived back at Dewsfold Jenny felt
that her equilibrium had been restored, and she pushed
Fiona d'Arc to the back of her mind. Then Amanda
whispered something to her mother, and Sheila whooped
with delight.

'*Engaged*? Really? Well, they've taken their time, I

must say! Did you hear that, Dennis? These love-birds have made up their minds at last!'

'Yes, well, Amanda caught me kissing her, and it was the only excuse I could think of,' explained Findlay, looking wicked, though Jenny threw him a mildly reproachful look.

There were congratulations, kisses and embraces as Findlay was wholeheartedly welcomed into the family, much to Jenny's satisfaction.

'Tomorrow we *have* to go and tell my parents, darling, and the day after that I'll take you back to Stretbury and tell Grannie and Grampy and everybody else!'

After the rapturous response of the Curtises to their news, Jenny allowed herself to be persuaded. With her head on his shoulder, she told herself that there was no need to be apprehensive with this man at her side.

'I simply can't believe what I'm hearing.'

Mrs d'Arc's face had gone white, and Henri tried in vain to reason with her.

'But can you not see that our son is happy, *ma chérie*? Happier than at any time since—'

'It won't last, Henri. He has been carried away on a tide of emotional sentiment, and by the time he sees he has made a mistake he—'

'Mother! Papa! Stop talking about me as if I were a child or a half-wit and listen to me, will you?' ordered Findlay. 'When I first met Jenny in April I knew that she was the only woman for me, if she would have me, and—'

'Not much doubt of *that*,' muttered Mrs d'Arc under her breath.

'Right, Mother, I shall not stay to hear my future wife

insulted. Come, Jenny, I'm very sorry about this but we're leaving.'

It was not the anger but the pain she saw in his eyes that gave Jenny courage.

'Not so fast, Findlay. *I* have something to say,' she interposed, sitting down and speaking as clearly and as calmly as she could.

'Now, Mrs d'Arc, I know exactly how you feel because you told me when I first met you. I respect your devotion to Gabriella's memory, but I want to assure you that I have no intention of taking her place. I couldn't, in any case. She was completely different from me. I know that there can never be another woman like her in Findlay's life but I'm quite willing to accept second place, and I hope very much that I shall be able to give him children, which I know he wants more than anything.

'If you can accept me on these terms there's no need for a rift between you and Findlay. That's not what I want.'

Mrs d'Arc put out an arm to keep her balance as she lowered herself into a chair. All of a sudden she seemed older and frailer, and when she spoke her voice quavered a little.

'When is this marriage supposed to take place?' she asked.

'At Christmas,' replied Jenny. 'Your son would like it to be earlier, but I have said he has until Christmas to change his mind.'

'Jenny!' broke in Findlay. 'I absolutely refuse to wait that long.'

She turned her flushed face to him, her eyes defiantly bright.

'I'm afraid you'll have to, Findlay, in view of what your mother has said. I hope she'll at least give me credit for being honest with her.'

At that moment Henri came over and seized Jenny's hand.

'You are just what my son needs, Jenny. So long have I hoped for somebody like you to come into his life. *Bienvenue*!'

Turning to his wife, he addressed her with gentle firmness.

'*Alors*! Fiona, will you now give us tea? If you do not, Findlay will take Jenny away and we may not see them again for a very long time. And I shall retire to my study for the rest of the day. The choice is yours.'

Fiona d'Arc took a couple of deep breaths, and struggled within herself. 'Very well,' she said at last. 'Tea will be served on the terrace in fifteen minutes, Miss—er—Jenny.'

'Thank you, Fiona. That's most kind of you,' replied Jenny promptly.

Although conversation over the cucumber sandwiches and cake was not particularly easy, all four of them made an effort. Jenny described the various places of local interest that she had been shown, and Henri said he was surprised that Findlay had not taken her to see the watermill.

'It was in a state of dereliction until it was restored by a group of enthusiasts, Jenny. You must make sure that Findlay takes you there before you leave.'

On the whole, Jenny thought that she had acquitted herself well. If it had not exactly been a knock-out victory, it was at least a win on points. She felt quite faint with relief as she parted from Fiona and Henri with a dutiful kiss.

Findlay's praise and gratefulness was sweet music in her ears as they drove out of Lyme.

'I can't part with you yet on such a lovely evening, Jenny,' he said they passed through a pretty village where a stream curved round a meadow in which sheep were grazing. 'You remember the old mill that Papa mentioned? This is a good opportunity to show it to you.'

He stopped the car beside a farm gate, and led her through into a field and along a footpath beside a tall hedgerow. Daisies and campion grew here in profusion, and the air was warm and still in the afterglow of a hot summer's day.

'Papa belongs to the preservation society that restored the mill,' said Findlay as they came in sight of the ancient building with its great wheel beside the running stream. 'It hasn't been in use since the last century, but I picture it as a centre of activity when farmers brought their grain in horse-drawn waggons to be ground into flour.'

'Let's sit here for a while, and you can tell me all about it,' said Jenny, sinking down in the long grass. He willingly obeyed, putting an arm around her and drawing her head onto his shoulder.

Jenny thought there was nowhere in the world she would rather be. There was no sound but the muted bird-song of evening and the chirp of a cricket on the sweet, meadow-scented air. Findlay stretched himself out at full length, drawing her down beside him. After a moment or two she raised herself to look at him as he lay with

his eyes closed, a little smile playing at the corners of
his mouth.

All tension, all perplexity had gone. The lines on his
face were softened, and he breathed utter contentment.
How good he was to look upon! Jenny put out a hand
to touch his face, running her forefinger down his forehead and nose, circling his mouth, tracing every contour
with the freedom that his love gave her.

Findlay…Findlay d'Arc. Could it be possible that this
man—so eminent in his profession, respected at home
and abroad, who had practised in the capitals of Europe
and amongst the poor and obscure—was the same man
who was lying here beside her now in a rural idyll?

His eyes opened.

'Jenny.'

'Yes, Findlay?' She lay down beside him again, but
he raised himself on one elbow and looked down at her
upturned face.

'There was something you said to my mother which
wasn't true, you know. I've been wanting to correct you
ever since.'

'Go on. What was it?'

'Forgive me, but it was when you mentioned
Gabriella. About you taking second place to her.'

Jenny hesitated. 'I said that to your mother, Findlay,
knowing her devotion to Gabriella's memory. And, after
all, she *was* the first love of your life, and I know that
you'll never forget what she meant to you—'

She was cut short by two long fingers laid upon her
lips.

'Bless you, darling Jenny, don't ever think of yourself
as second-best. I loved Gabriella, but that was another
time. I've changed, Jenny, and it's *you* now—the girl

who's come into my life and changed me—can't you see? Oh, Jenny, Jenny! If you only knew how much I've dreamed of you, loving you—oh, *Jenny*!'

She was unable to speak for the joy that welled up in her heart. Their lips met in a long, wordless kiss, and then he buried his dark head against her neck, kissing her throat and pulling aside her dress to kiss her shoulder.

With shaking hands she undid the buttons that fastened the dress front, and he slipped his arms around her beneath it. She felt her bra being unhooked, and then gasped with delight as her eager breasts were cupped and caressed in his hands. His uprush of desire caused an immediate response in her own body—it was like a fire surging through their veins.

'Findlay, love me, love me,' she breathed.

'Jenny—it—it's not really private enough here,' he muttered. 'Somebody might be out taking the dog for a walk! But, look, there's the mill. And—and Papa put the key into my hand when we left,' he confessed.

'Ah, Findlay, so you knew what would happen—'

'I knew it might happen, Jenny. Do you mind?'

For answer she let him lead her to the thick wooden door and into the silent building, which had once been such a hive of industry and now slept beside the stream, wrapped in its dreams of the past.

The deep shade of the interior beneath the massive wooden beams revealed a bewildering assortment of cogs and pulleys, draped with sagging chains and ropes, and on the far wall a wooden staircase led to the second storey where the millstones lay between chutes and hoppers and all the mysterious paraphernalia of the milling trade.

Findlay led her up this stairway and then another, which brought them to the top room where the evening light filtered in through two small windows. The bare boards of the floor were clean and dry, and there was some sacking piled in a corner. Findlay took off his jacket to roll up and make a pillow for her.

What happened next seemed as natural as it was inevitable. His sheer physical need, so long kept in submission, would no longer be denied, and she was eager and willing. Their clothes were quickly discarded, and his kisses upon her warm flesh were beyond any bliss she had imagined. She trembled and sighed with pleasure. He gently fingered the scar that he himself had made, and softly touched it with his lips before he carefully stretched his long body upon her.

Like a thirsty traveller who has at last found an oasis of water, like a starving man faced with wholesome bread to eat, Findlay rejoiced in the body of this woman who was so happy for him to claim her as his own. She gave an exclamation of joy as she felt the weight of his body, gripping him with her knees, welcoming him between her thighs. She flung back her head with a stifled cry as she received him within her, deeply and deeper still... It happened so quickly that they were both taken by surprise.

'It's so simple, Jenny, so easy, my love, my...' His words became incoherent as he approached fulfilment.

'I know, Findlay, I know.' Her hands gripped his shoulders as they journeyed, arriving together at a soaring peak of exultation where for a timeless moment they were one with the earth, the sky, the summer evening and all creation. It seemed to Jenny that her body was dissolving in the heat of his passion, and she found that her face was wet with tears.

'I love you, Jenny—oh, how I love you, love you.'

Slowly, slowly he released his hold on her. Gradually their breathing slowed, their bodies softened and relaxed. They lay peacefully together in a long, sweetly satisfying aftermath, and an enormous contentment spread over them. All doubts and misgivings were at an end, all jealousies and misunderstandings consumed in that blazing union of body, mind and spirit.

Jenny was no longer worried about Fiona d'Arc. Findlay's possession of her had raised her to a new status, and she knew that she need never be haunted by memories of the past. As she lay in his encircling arms she resolved to work very hard at establishing a good relationship with her future mother-in-law, who would now have to face the truth that her son had the same basic and natural desires as other men.

And Jenny intended to fulfil them.

The news of their engagement was greeted with happy congratulations at Stretbury Memorial, though not with a great deal of surprise. Even Lady Hylton had seen the devotion Mr d'Arc had shown to Sister Curtis after her operation. Jenny's many friends were glad for her, and if some were a little envious, like Heather Hulland, it was swallowed up in an abundance of goodwill. And, of course, her grandparents were overjoyed.

'Now we shan't have to worry about you any more, Jenny, dear,' said Grannie happily. 'We know you've got a good man to look after you when we've gone!'

They decided that Findlay's Bristol flat would do for a first home, but he was deeply touched when Grampy drew him aside and told him that Bailey's Cottage was left jointly to Jenny and Dennis, but that Findlay would be able to purchase Dennis's share and then it would be the matrimonial home of Mr and Mrs Findlay d'Arc.

'Dennis'll be glad to sell out to you, Doctor. He's told me,' confided Grampy. 'Been in the family for two hundred years, this place, and Doris and me 'ud like to think of you and Jenny living in it, and your children growing up here.'

Everybody wanted to know the date of the wedding, and Jenny said that she had fixed on Christmas to give them time to make all the essential readjustments and necessary preparations. Findlay made a face and openly declared that she had no right to torment him with such a long wait. It became something of a joke among their friends, and then all of a sudden the matter was settled.

One evening towards the end of September, after a day in which both of them had been working at full stretch, they decided to buy a fish-and-chip supper and take it to Findlay's flat. Sitting opposite each other at his little dining table, they tucked in with good appetites.

'What do you want for your birthday, Findlay?' Jenny asked, holding up a chip on the end of her fork.

'A nice early wedding,' he replied promptly, sprinkling salt and vinegar liberally over his plate.

Jenny ignored this. 'Would you like a comprehensive illustrated guide to English architecture, something that would include houses like Bailey's Cottage and places like—er—old water-mills?' she asked innocently. 'Or I'd thought of a box of blank video tapes to record all the programmes you're never in to watch. There's one about the British coastline next week—just up your street.'

'That's sweet of you, Jenny, but you've taken away the element of surprise now, haven't you?' he teased.

'Oh, yes, so I have. Still,' she went on, spearing a juicy morsel of cod, 'I think I've got something that *will* be a surprise for you, Findlay.'

'What's that, darling? Mmm, this batter is really good.'

'If you could just take your mind off your stomach for half a minute, Mr d'Arc, I'll tell you—that is, if you really want to know.'

She tried to sound casual, but there was a little tremor of excitement in her voice that made him look up quickly.

'Jenny, what is it? Tell me, my darling, don't keep me in suspense!'

She didn't answer, and he looked into her eyes with growing concern. And he saw the truth.

With a shout he leapt up from the table.

'Jenny! Oh, *Jenny*, you're—you're—'

'Yes, Findlay, in May. I didn't want to tell you until I was sure, but I missed my September period and started feeling a bit off so I did a test. Oh, Findlay, be careful!'

For he had seized her in his arms and lifted her off her chair.

'Jenny, my little angel! This is the most wonderful news, the best birthday present in the world—dearest, dearest Jenny!'

He began to gallop round the room with her in an improvised version of the can-can.

'Findlay, stop it! You don't want the whole block to know,' she protested, laughing.

'Yes, I do, I want *everybody* to know that I'm going

to be a papa—and no more nonsense about Christmas now. We'll get married next week!'

'Actually, Findlay, I thought the end of October would be ideal for a nice, quiet wedding at Stretbury Parish Church, with just family and friends.'

'In which case, it'll be packed out,' he grinned.

'And Findlay...'

'Yes, my darling?'

'There is just one thing.'

'What's that, Jenny?'

'How are you going to tell your mother?'

He stared at her open-mouthed, and she could hardly keep a straight face. He gave a low whistle.

'Good heavens!' exclaimed Mr Findlay d'Arc.

As it happened, Fiona d'Arc did not need to be told. She diagnosed the three-month pregnancy herself, not by anything that was said but because of the overwhelming joy that showed in everything her son said and did. His father took him aside to congratulate him privately.

'Fiona tells me that there must be a good reason for bringing forward the happy day,' he said with all the pride of a future grandfather. 'Did you find the keys of use to you, *mon fils*? You will regard *le moulin* with a special affection in future, yes?'

Findlay was proved right about the packed church and the number of friends, colleagues and ex-patients who came to see Mr d'Arc married to Sister Curtis. The bride slowed her steps as she took her grandfather's arm to walk up the aisle in a cream silk dress cut in the Empire style that suited her so well, her face framed by a pretty straw hat trimmed with golden chrysanthemums.

A shaft of autumn sunlight fell upon the couple as

they made their vows, and as soon as they were declared man and wife the bridegroom claimed a kiss at the altar, in the face of the congregation.

For Jenny's grandparents it was a very special day, and reunited them with their daughter, Cathy, who had flown over from New South Wales to see her eldest daughter married. It had been Jenny's idea to invite her mother to be present on this most important of occasions. Findlay had willingly helped with Cathy's air fare, and was rewarded by the tearful embrace between the bride and her long-absent mother, a moment of forgiveness and healing of past bitterness.

'It's been the crowning touch, Jenny, to see you reconciled with your mother,' he said as they stood welcoming their guests at the reception. 'Look at her over there, talking to Dennis and Sheila and the children—and there's Grampy introducing her to his young friend, Andrew, and telling her about the job the lad's got with Stretbury Parks Department, thanks to good old Lady Hylton!'

Hanging on her husband's arm and smiling as each new guest arrived, young Mrs d'Arc looked the very picture of happiness, as all her friends agreed, but Findlay was taken aside by his mother and told not to let his wife over-exert herself.

'Fetch a chair for her, Findlay. She has been standing for too long and will be tired,' warned the old lady. 'You should know better with a woman in her—er—'

'What's that for?' asked Jenny when he appeared with a chair.

'My mother feels that I'm not taking proper care of her grandchild,' he explained.

'Oh, bless her! Then I'd better sit down, hadn't I?' laughed the bride, and looked so charming that he had to kiss her again.

MILLS & BOON®

Elizabeth Gage

The Collection

A compelling read of three full-length novels by best-selling author of *A Glimpse of Stocking*

Intimate

Number One

A Stranger to Love

"...Gage is a writer of style and intelligence..."
—Chicago Tribune

On sale from 13th July 1998   Price £5.25

Available at most branches of WH Smith, John Menzies, Martins, Tesco, Asda, and Volume One

SPOT THE DIFFERENCE

Spot all ten differences between the two pictures featured below and you could win a year's supply of Mills & Boon® books—FREE! When you're finished, simply complete the coupon overleaf and send it to us by 31st December 1998. The first five correct entries will each win a year's subscription to the Mills & Boon series of their choice. What could be easier?

Please turn over for details of how to enter ⇨ F8C

HOW TO ENTER

Simply study the two pictures overleaf. They may at first glance appear the same but look closely and you should start to see the differences. There are ten to find in total, so circle them as you go on the second picture. Finally, fill in the coupon below and pop this page into an envelope and post it today. Don't forget you could win a year's supply of Mills & Boon® books—you don't even need to pay for a stamp!

Mills & Boon Spot the Difference Competition FREEPOST CN81, Croydon, Surrey, CR9 3WZ
EIRE readers: (please affix stamp) PO Box 4546, Dublin 24.

Please tick the series you would like to receive if you are one of the lucky winners

Presents™ ❑ Enchanted™ ❑ Medical Romance™ ❑
Historical Romance™ ❑ Temptation® ❑

Are you a Reader Service™ subscriber?   Yes ❑   No ❑

Ms/Mrs/Miss/Mr ....Initials ....
(BLOCK CAPITALS PLEASE)

Surname...

Address ....

....

....Postcode...........................

(I am over 18 years of age)   F8C

Closing date for entries is 31st December 1998.
One application per household. Competition open to residents of the UK and Ireland only. You may be mailed with offers from other reputable companies as a result of this application. If you would prefer not to receive such offers, please tick this box. ❑

Mills & Boon is a registered trademark owned by Harlequin Mills & Boon Limited.

MILLS & BOON®

Medical Romance™

COMING NEXT MONTH

HERO'S LEGACY by Margaret Barker

Jackie had never expected to feel like this again and it was great! She realised that she'd been living in the past and now Tom was going to help her face the future.

FORSAKING ALL OTHERS by Laura MacDonald

Book 3 of the Matchmaker quartet

Siobhan thought that David was gorgeous but a playboy. If he wanted her he'd have to prove he was serious—it was marriage or nothing!

TAKE ONE BACHELOR by Jennifer Taylor

Could this gorgeous woman really be his new assistant? But Matthew wasn't tempted, after all he'd just decided to steer clear of women, hadn't he?

A MATTER OF PRACTICE by Helen Shelton

Kids and Kisses...another heart-warming story

The birth of their son and their heavy work-load had put a lot of strain on Claire and Ben's marriage. Ben was sure they could work it out but could he convince Claire?

On sale from 13th July 1998

Available at most branches of WH Smith, John Menzies, Martins, Tesco, Volume One and Safeway

COLLECTOR'S EDITION

The *Penny Jordan Collector's Edition* is
a selection of her most popular stories,
published in beautifully designed volumes
for you to collect and cherish.

*Available from Tesco, Asda, WH Smith, John Menzies,
Martins and all good paperback stockists, at £3.10 each -
or the special price of £2.80 if you use the coupon below.
On sale from 1st June 1998.*

Valid only in the UK & Eire against purchases made in retail outlets and not in
conjunction with any Reader Service or other offer.

30ᵖ OFF
COUPON
VALID UNTIL: 31.8.1998
PENNY JORDAN COLLECTOR'S EDITION

To the Customer: This coupon can be used in part payment for a
copy of PENNY JORDAN COLLECTOR'S EDITION. Only one
coupon can be used against each copy purchased. Valid only in the
UK & Eire against purchases made in retail outlets and not in
conjunction with any Reader Service or other offer. Please do not
attempt to redeem this coupon against any other product as refusal
to accept may cause embarrassment and delay at the checkout.

To the Retailer: Harlequin Mills & Boon will redeem this coupon at
face value provided only that it has been taken in part payment for
any book in the PENNY JORDAN COLLECTOR'S EDITION. The
company reserves the right to refuse payment against misredeemed
coupons. Please submit coupons to: Harlequin Mills & Boon Ltd.
NCH Dept 730, Corby, Northants NN17 1NN.

9 904170 250306 >

0472 01316